I0838492

THE HORSE MISTRESS:
BOOK 1

Other books by R. A. Steffan

The Complete Horse Mistress Collection
The Complete Lion Mistress Collection
The Complete Dragon Mistress Collection

Circle of Blood: Books 1-3
Circle of Blood: Books 4-6
(with Jaelynn Woolf)

The Last Vampire: Books 1-3
The Last Vampire: Books 4-6
(with Jaelynn Woolf)

Vampire Bound: Complete Series, Books 1-4

Forsaken Fae: The Complete Series, Books 1-3

Antidote: Love and War, Book 1
Antigen: Love and War, Book 2
Antibody: Love and War, Book 3
Anthelion: Love and War, Book 4
Antagonist: Love and War, Book 5

Diamond Bar Apha Ranch
Diamond Bar Alpha 2: Angel & Vic
(with Jaelynn Woolf)

THE HORSE MISTRESS:
BOOK 1

R. A. STEFFAN

The Horse Mistress: Book 1

Copyright 2015 by OtherLove Publishing, LLC

All rights reserved. Printed in the United States of America. No part of this book may be used or reproduced in any manner whatsoever without written permission except in the case of brief quotations embedded in critical articles or reviews.

This book is a work of fiction. Names, characters, businesses, organizations, places, events and incidents either are the product of the author's imagination or are used fictitiously. Any resemblance to actual persons, living or dead, events, or locales is entirely coincidental.

ISBN: 978-1-955073-19-6 (paperback)

For information, contact the author at
http://www.rasteffan.com/contact/

Cover art by Deranged Doctor Design

Third Edition: January 2022

Author's Note

This book contains descriptions of graphic sex, including sex between men, and sex with multiple partners. Additionally, it deals with issues of gender identity and gender fluidity. It is intended for a mature audience.

Table of Contents

ONE

"Carivel! Where are you, boy? Come here at once!"

The voice of Jorun, the old Horse Master, was gruff and impatient as it rang out across the dusty horse pens. I looked up from the section of fence I was mending, quickly locating the short figure striding toward me with his distinctive, bow-legged gait.

"Here, Horse Master," I called in reply. I gathered up my tools and placed them safely outside the fence so the animals wouldn't step on them, before hurrying across to meet him halfway.

"Aren't you done with those repairs yet?" Jorun asked, his piercing, deep-set eyes raking over me from within his weathered face.

"Almost, sir," I said.

"Quick as you can, then. I want you to watch over that buckskin mare of Volya's tonight. She's finally ready to foal."

I nodded my understanding. Volya's favorite mare had delivered a creamy white colt last year—a rare prize indeed. The village chief had high hopes that she would throw a matching foal this year, so he could have a white chariot team the envy of every warrior for miles around. Mares were generally left to give birth on their own whilst out with the herd, but for this particular foal nothing would be left to chance.

"Of course, Horse Master," I said. "I'll finish up here and be back at dusk."

"Good, good," said Jorun. "Mind you eat something first, lad. Being hungry is one thing. Being tired is another. Being hungry and tired at the same time will have you falling asleep before the moon finishes rising."

"I'll get something from Gretya, sir. Thank you."

"See that you do." Jorun patted my shoulder firmly with a gnarled hand. "Maybe someday you'll actually get some meat on those bones."

I resolutely held in the sigh that wanted to escape—I wasn't *that* skinny. *Honestly.* I might not be tall or broad-shouldered, but I was certainly more than strong enough to do my job as Jorun's apprentice. However, that didn't seem to stop the man from fussing as though he were my father and not my master.

After mumbling some vague words of agreement, I returned to the final section of fence. One of the rails was rotting where it attached to the post, so I pried it free and replaced it with a new one, pausing to shoo away a curious yearling that wandered up to sniff at my close-cropped hair. Job done, I tidied everything up, wheeling the debris away in a rickety wooden pushcart.

The pens were located a short distance beyond the edges of the main part of the settlement, so that the flies and the smell of manure would not be a nuisance to the residents. The sun was already getting low in the sky when I returned to the center of the village and entered Gretya's cookhouse. The thatched, circular structure was generally a hub of activity in the evenings, and today was no exception. The late spring weather was pleasant; several men and boys were already lounging on the benches scattered around the outside of the building with their bowls of hearty stew, while Gretya's daughters flitted back and forth between the tables, filling tankards.

Gretya was a widow, and made a living serving food to those who were unable or unwilling to cook for themselves, for whatever reason. I couldn't afford to eat meals here very often with my meager apprentice's pay, but every once in a while I had reason to appreciate the availability of her hearty fare. Tonight was definitely one of those nights, since I would soon need to return to the horse pens for my watch.

"Hello, Carivel, dear," said the old woman, giving me a gap-toothed smile as she ladled meat and vegetables into a bowl. The rich aroma made my stomach rumble, causing her smile to widen. "I don't see you nearly often enough, you know. You're looking well these days."

I gave her an answering smile of my own. "Hello, Gretya. If you can convince Jorun to double my pay, I promise I'll darken your doorstep every day of the week. My own cooking always tastes like I forgot to add the salt, even when I didn't."

"Ah, you poor lad. I'll have a quiet word with the old miser one day soon and see what can be done," she said with a wink.

4

I laughed softly before thanking her and taking my leave. The village gossips all swore blind that Gretya was Jorun's mistress, an idea that she playfully encouraged, but which had never to my knowledge been proven one way or the other. On those rare occasions when someone was foolish enough to bring up the question within Jorun's hearing, they were treated to a stony glare and an even stonier silence. Personally, I was firmly in the "yes" camp—I found something appealing about the idea of the grizzled old grouch secretly doting on such a sweet, motherly figure.

With a quick glance around the yard outside the cookhouse, I identified several of the other boys who helped with the horses chatting amiably among themselves. More interestingly, Senovo was deep in conversation with one of the village elders on the farthest bench, his partially shaved head and the dun-colored robes of a novice priest distinctive in the early evening light. His smooth, handsome face was grim.

I dithered for a moment over asking to join them before losing my nerve and moving to a table several feet away from the pair, but still close enough that I could hear them talking.

Coward, I berated myself.

"Volya won't give in to some tin-plated Alyrion field marshal who thinks he can come in with a pack of soldiers and trample our way of life," the older man was saying. "He'll send them back where they came from with an earful."

"I do hope you're right," Senovo said mildly. "However, I fear it may not be quite that simple."

Volya, the chief of the village, had ridden out four days ago with a small party of warriors, replying to a summons from an Alyrion commander—newly arrived from the mainland—who demanded a parlay. Eburos was an island rich in resources, but it had only really gained the attention of the powerful Alyrion Empire within the last year or two. It probably helped that Eburos was protected by the sea on all sides, but it seemed that the lure of our fertile soil and productive mines had finally overcome the emperor's reluctance to send troops across the water.

Now, the collection of small, disorganized tribes and villages that called the island home found themselves facing a powerful foe. Some tribes in the south had already capitulated without even attempting to muster a defense, but as the Alyrions moved north into areas like Draebard, they would quickly discover that not all Eburosi were so accommodating.

"I understand Volya took Andoc with him," said the elder, causing my ears to perk up even further at the mention of Senovo's close friend. "He thinks a lot of that young man, you know. Wouldn't surprise me if the Chief was grooming him as a replacement, what with Volya losing his only son last year."

"Andoc has many enviable qualities... for a warrior," Senovo replied, a wry note entering his voice. "However, I'm not certain that the patience required for leadership is among them."

I hid my derisive snort; the man across from Senovo didn't bother hiding his. Everyone in the village knew that the young priest and Andoc were virtually inseparable. Their mutual regard appeared to know no bounds despite their tendency to tease and belittle each other at every opportunity. And oh, how I envied them that easy camaraderie — the close bond between two people that I would never, ever be able to have. Instead, I was reduced to watching them both with secretive, longing glances... daydreaming about their perfect features... about Senovo's voice like melting honey, Andoc's broad shoulders and strong arms.

My wistful thoughts — not to mention my eavesdropping — were interrupted by the arrival of Gretya's youngest daughter with a pitcher of ale.

"Hello, Limdya," I said politely, forcing down a wince as she blushed and smiled at me with sparkling eyes.

"Hello, Carivel!" she replied. "Some of the others are saying that Volya's mare might have another white foal tonight. Is that true?"

"Yes, it's true. The Horse Master ordered me to keep watch over her, so he must think the foal is finally coming." I hoped that would be the end of it, but of course it wasn't.

"How exciting!" she said. "I wish I could see a new foal being born. Maybe I could come out and watch with you later?"

"I'm sorry, Limdya," I said with as much regret as I could muster. "But you know women aren't allowed to help with the horses. It's bad luck, and the gods might retaliate by making the foal stillborn."

The words seemed to stick in my throat, but at least they did the job even if they made me feel queasy. Limdya's face fell in disappointment.

"Oh. Well, I wouldn't want to risk that, of course. Perhaps you could come over to the house tomorrow morning and I'll cook breakfast for you? You could tell me all about it then. My cooking is almost as good as Mother's, you know," she added hopefully.

The queasy feeling continued to grow despite the excellent stew I'd been eating. "I'm afraid all I'll be interested in tomorrow morning is a few hours' sleep, Limdya. Perhaps another time."

The sparkle was completely gone from the girl's eyes, and she seemed to slump in on herself slightly. "Yes," she said. "Another time."

"Don't take it so personal, love," called one of the boys from the other bench. It was Dalon, of course... always a thorn in my side. "Carivel here, he never looks twice at any of the girls. Thinks himself above all of you — too good for the likes of a village lass."

"That's not true," I said quietly, trying to catch Limdya's eyes as the others at the table laughed. She wouldn't meet my gaze, and my stomach churned harder.

"He saves his lingering looks for Andoc," Dalon carried on. "He'd probably rather be taken like a maiden by a big, strong warrior than be the one doing the taking."

Oh, the irony. If he only knew.

"Who knows," said one of the others. "Andoc might even go for it. He likes eunuchs well enough, and our Carivel looks sort of like a eunuch with his smooth face and narrow shoulders. Don't you think so, Limdya?"

"Very funny, you two," I said. "You know perfectly well that I had a girl in my old village. She died of a fever, and I still miss her too much to even think about being with another woman."

The old story—the old lie—came as easily as ever. There was a bit of quiet guffawing from Dalon's table, but at least Limdya's expression transformed into one of sympathy rather than hurt before she left quietly to serve the other patrons. A cool hand closed on my shoulder a moment later, startling me. I looked up sharply at the figure behind me.

Senovo. My heart sped up.

"A very noble sentiment, Carivel," said the novice priest, and the boys at the other table suddenly found a great deal of interest in their bowls of food. "Surely, though, your lost love would not want you to be alone forever."

I forced myself to meet Senovo's green-gold eyes. To speak calmly, as if my heart were not fluttering against my ribcage like a trapped bird. "Perhaps not."

He held my gaze for a long moment, and arched one dark eyebrow. "Ah well," he said. "You are still young, after all. Barely even a man. There's plenty of time."

In truth, I was roughly the same age as Senovo. The same age as Andoc. As for the rest of it, though…

"I should get ready for my watch tonight," I said.

"Of course. May the gods smile on your endeavors," Senovo said. The hand that had been resting on my shoulder moved to touch my forehead in a brief blessing before he smiled and moved away. My skin tingled where his fingers had brushed against me.

As I rose and tidied away my half-finished bowl, I caught Dalon smirking at me out of the corner of my eye.

In the privacy and safety of my tiny, ramshackle hut, I took a few minutes to flop down on the straw mattress in the corner and just breathe. I had maintained my secret—my ruse—for almost three years now. I wouldn't slip up now, just because Senovo was kind to me and smiled down at me with lazy green eyes.

Though it's not unheard of for a man to lie with a beautiful eunuch, said a little voice in my head, ever so unhelpfully. But… there was also Andoc.

I sighed and stripped my dusty tunic over my head, exposing the soft leather wrappings that bound my breasts to make my chest appear flat. As I unwrapped myself, pausing now and then to scrape ragged fingernails over the itchy places where the leather had chafed, I contemplated the hopelessness of my situation.

Through some cruel joke of the gods, I was born a girl. I never fit in as one, though—no matter how much my mother wished it. I was fascinated by the horse pens in my childhood village almost from the time I could walk, and railed against the restrictions prohibiting women from tending the animals.

The gods gave men and women different roles, I was told repeatedly by the village priests, after every childish infraction. *Only male spirits are strong enough to control the spirits of animals. They cannot thrive under the care of a woman. If you want to take care of living things, perhaps you should consider becoming a healer, or a grower of plants?*

I still remember the tears of frustration, carefully hidden from all who might see and judge me for them, after trying to tell the priests that my spirit was more male than female. It just happened to be hidden inside the body of a slender girl child. Watching the girls my age as I grew up was like looking at something foreign, something… *other*. Sometimes it felt as though the only thing I had inherited from my sex was a love of attractive men.

Not that it mattered much, at this point. Even had my attraction been for women, to get close to another person in such a way would be to betray my secret. A man would not want me because I dressed and acted like a boy. Even if I found someone who loved other men — a practice more or less tolerated between a man and a eunuch, but taboo between two un-castrated men — such a person would not want me because my body was still that of a woman. I was destined to be alone, and to make things even worse, my heart had fixated on two utterly unattainable people who already had each other and would certainly have no interest in me.

Perhaps it was safer that way.

Tossing the breast bindings aside, I reached for the clay pot of beeswax and tallow that I used to soothe my skin, rubbing it in and letting the pleasant sensation soothe my nerves. My breasts were thankfully small, but today they were still tender as I suffered through the tail end of my moon cycle. Pulling down my breeches, my lip curled in distaste as I pulled out the pad of rabbit fur wrapped in a linen rag that I used to staunch the flow of blood.

The bleeding had slowed since yesterday, which was good since I had no more rabbit fur and didn't have the time to go searching for moss or some other absorbent material this evening. I rinsed out the linen rag in a bucket of well water and folded it back into a square. It would have to be enough.

Dusk was fading into dark when I arrived back at the pens beyond the village outskirts. Volya's mare had been given her own small corral somewhat away from the other horses, but still within sight. A three-sided shelter stood in one corner, bedded with dried peat moss hauled in from a nearby bog. I approached the fence and held out a hand, palm-down, for the mare to sniff. Cassira was a sweet horse for the most part, but had displayed something of a fierce streak after foaling her first colt last year.

That was fine; it was a mother's job to protect her offspring, after all... something I wished my own mother had shown more of an inclination to do. After greeting the little horse and demonstrating that it wasn't my intent to sneak around and hide from her like a predator, I wandered off to find a comfortable post somewhere out of the way to lean against. With my blanket wrapped around my shoulders against the slight evening chill, and a waterskin at my side, I curled up so I could see the moonlight glinting off the horse's dappled buckskin coat. Leaning my head back against the thick, wooden post, I soaked in the faint warmth that emanated from it, left over from the day's bright sunlight.

Cassira wandered restlessly around the pen, stopping occasionally to pick up a mouthful of hay or stare across at the other horses dozing in their corral. A foal watch like this one was usually a recipe for utter boredom, and while I was aware of the level of trust Jorun was placing in me, that didn't make watching a horse walk around and eat hay over the course of several hours any more interesting. Before the full moon had reached a point halfway toward its zenith, my mind began to wander.

Because I apparently liked to torture myself, it turned fairly quickly to thoughts of Andoc and Senovo. During the summer months, Andoc had a habit of sparring with the other warriors wearing only a loincloth, which left little to the imagination when it came to his enviable physique. Senovo, though, was always clad in his robes, leaving quite a bit to the imagination. The priests—eunuchs, all of them—were softer than the warriors with their sinewy, battle-hardened bodies. Most eunuchs tended toward roundness through the belly, but not Senovo, whose features were fine and whose body was slender. His face was nearly as smooth as my own. The front half of his head was shaved close, while the straight, black hair growing from the back of his skull was braided into the single, heavy plait that all priests possessed.

For religious ceremonies, he always lined his eyes with kohl. The sight had never failed to captivate me for some reason.

I wondered what he and Andoc did together in private. The lads in the village had plenty to say on the matter, all of it coarse and much of it rather unlikely sounding, though as someone who had never lain with another person for fear of my birth sex being discovered, I suppose I wasn't in any real position to judge.

In my mind, they kissed passionately and stroked each other with loving fingers. I had a vague idea of what being a eunuch must entail, having seen dozens of colts castrated into geldings over the years. It seemed to me to be an exceedingly cruel thing to do to a human boy. Still, the geldings recovered well enough, and some of them even continued to mount mares afterward, though of course they could not sire foals. So, in my idle daydreams and fantasies, Senovo still gave and received pleasure, writhing with Andoc in a passionate tangle of lips and hands.

The night was quiet and my solitude complete. My left hand drifted up, sliding under my tunic to brush over my raw, sensitive nipples. Leaving my breasts unbound tonight was a calculated risk—but it was dark, and if I saw anybody, it would only be Jorun as I woke him to ask for help in case there was a problem with the foal that I couldn't deal with myself. He wouldn't notice if my chest seemed slightly less flat than usual. Though my breasts were a nuisance, there was no denying that touching them like this felt good. So good, in fact, that I felt a pulse of wetness between my legs.

I sighed, irritated, letting my head fall back against the post with a soft thump. I was still bleeding a bit, and had only a linen rag to catch it. If I wasn't careful, the mess would soak through my breeches.

Mood ruined, I pulled my hand out of my tunic and returned my full focus to the mare with her swollen, heavy belly. Cassira was still restless, pacing the fence. After a few minutes, she froze, looking out into the dark at a point slightly to the east of where I was sitting. With an explosive snort, she abruptly bolted to the far side of the pen, her pendulous belly swinging with every stride. In the large communal corral, the other horses stirred nervously and started to mill around.

I rose, cautious, and followed the fence until I could get a clear look at the open space beyond. Glowing, yellow-green eyes stared at me from out of the dark, and I caught my breath in surprise.

The moonlight illuminated thick gray fur and a sharply pointed white muzzle as a large wolf crept forward silently with smooth, deliberate steps, sniffing the air. The horses were charging back and forth in their pens now, the herd forming up in a tight ring with the youngsters in the middle. Cassira squealed and cantered back and forth along the section of fence I had repaired the previous afternoon, pausing to shove against the rails with her chest as she sought escape.

The hair on the back of my neck rose and a shiver traced its way down my spine at the thought of a wolf this close to the edge of the village. Had it sensed that the mare was about to give birth to a tender, vulnerable foal? For now, at least, the creature's attention seemed more focused on me than the horses, which was... well, both good and not so good, depending on how you looked at it. I tore my eyes from its glowing gaze to cast around my immediate surroundings in the moonlight. My attention caught on a scattering of fist-sized rocks near the fence, and I dropped into a crouch, picking up as many as I could hold.

I threw the first one as hard as I could at those slanted eyes. It missed, though not by much, and the wolf skittered a step to the side. A low growl rolled across the space between us. The second stone flew true, the growl ending in a yip as the rock hit the predator just above one glowing eye. It was already turning to run as my third rock thumped into its shoulder. The rustling sound of paws running through grass faded into the darkness, and I let out a breath I hadn't even realized I'd been holding.

Clammy sweat made me shiver as I turned to check on the horses. The herd was quieting, but Cassira still stood in the far corner, head high and ears pricked as she followed the sounds made by the retreating beast. There would be no foal tonight, with the mare now on high alert after the threat. I sighed. I would have to maintain my vigil regardless, lest the wolf return. And, of course, Jorun would have my head if I let something bad happen on my watch.

I gathered up a few more rocks, just in case, and returned to my spot against the post. While I didn't feel remotely tired just then, I knew I couldn't afford to let my guard down as the small hours of the night crept by. Resettling myself in a position that was comfortable—but not *too* comfortable—I rummaged for the worn leather satchel I'd brought with me and pulled out a damaged horsewhip, along with some leather thongs. Angling it so the moonlight hit the braided leather, I started unpicking the frayed section, pausing at intervals to check the horses and my surroundings for unwanted four-legged company.

I was just tying off the end of the intricately braided repairs to the lash some considerable time later when I heard noises coming from the far side of the village. At first the sounds made no sense. It was the middle of the night—who would be shouting and clanging around with such total disregard for people sleeping? Only when the shouting turned to screaming did my weary thoughts start to make sense of the situation, sending my heart hammering with sudden terror.

It was the sound of an attack.

TWO

This was wrong. This shouldn't be happening. Neighboring tribes and villages attacked each other sometimes; of course they did. But Draebard was not involved in any disputes at the moment. There were no blood feuds or water shortages causing friction in the area. Besides, no self-respecting Eburosi warrior would *ever* countenance such a cowardly attack on a village in the middle of the night. It was beyond dishonorable. The gods would strike down any tribe that tried such a thing with a plague of boils, or worse.

I had been frozen in place with shock, but now I clambered to my feet and silently made my way back to the edge of the village, keeping close to fences and walls. I had to see what was happening. The screams were horrible, and as I approached I saw flickering light and smelled thick, greasy smoke. Whoever it was had set fire to some of the huts on the far side of the settlement.

I made my way closer to the center of the village and peeked around the edge of the wall I was hiding behind. Moonlight and orange firelight illuminated the strange, silvery metal chest armor favored by Alyrion soldiers as the figures pressed further into the village in orderly ranks. There looked to be at least three dozen men, armed with swords, pikes and torches.

Oh, gods. They'd drawn Volya and his retinue of warriors away from the settlement, and now they were attacking. Did they mean to kill us all and burn it to the ground, or was this supposed to be some sort of lesson? A warning to other Eburosi?

The horses.

They would steal the horses, or slaughter them. I turned and ran back toward the pens as fast as I could, all thoughts of stealth abandoned. My lungs were burning—as much with fear as with exhaustion—when I reached the gate of the first pen and threw it open. Cassira snorted, trotting through the gap in the fence and making straight for the rest of the herd, which was still milling around in the largest corral. I followed her as fast as I could and opened that gate as well, entering the pen and skirting along the fence to get behind the herd so I could drive them out.

"*Hyaah!*" I shouted, herding the animals through the gate and away from the village, along the track that led north, toward the summer pastures and the foothills beyond. Within seconds, the mob of horses had accelerated into a panicked gallop, the thunder of their hooves slowly fading beneath the sounds of the battle behind me as they disappeared into the distance.

The wolf had better watch himself, I thought, slightly hysterically. *He'll be trampled in the stampede if he's not careful.*

With the horses as safe as they could be under the circumstances, I hurried back to the post I'd been resting against to grab the horsewhip, then ran toward the village, and the screaming.

In my absence, the remaining warriors who had not gone with Volya had stumbled out of their huts, with swords, spears, and axes in their hands. Their furious battle cries echoed through the village. It was strangely jarring to see Eburosi warriors fighting in whatever clothing they'd been sleeping in, without any war paint smeared across their bodies or faces. Unadorned skin made them no less fierce, however, and the Alyrions' steady progress through the village was slowed as they engaged with the defenders.

Looking around, my attention was caught by a single armor-clad soldier with a torch, moving purposefully toward the cookhouse. Without stopping to think, I ran forward and let fly with the long-tailed lash of the horsewhip, aiming for the man's eyes. When he cried out and dropped the torch in favor of clawing at his face, I bared my teeth in what might have been vicious satisfaction. It was short-lived, however, as another soldier saw me. He closed in even as I tried to back away, sword in hand and anger twisting his face.

I cracked the whip again, aiming for the sword in hopes that I could pull it out of his hand. I missed, though, wrapping the lash around his forearm instead. He hissed at the sting, but immediately used it to drag me forward, off-balance and staggering. Before I could right myself, the pommel of his sword swept up toward my face. Pain exploded in my temple where it hit me and I dropped like a stone, ears ringing. Through blurry, wavering vision, I saw the flash of the blade as he lifted it for the killing stroke.

This is it, then, I thought, feeling surprisingly calm about the whole thing as my awareness flickered in and out, in time with my pounding heart.

Just as the blade began its downward arc, a large, gray shape slammed into the soldier, knocking him to the dirt with a cry. The wolf snarled, tearing at the man's throat, scarlet liquid soaking its jaws as I struggled to make sense of the scene before me through eyes that wouldn't focus properly. The red stain seemed to spread in my vision, reaching out to meet the soft, gray fog that was swirling inward from the periphery. I slipped into darkness with every expectation that I would never wake again.

When I did wake, sunlight was stabbing into my eyes. My skull throbbed in time with my heartbeat. I tried to groan in pain, but it emerged as a dry croak. An answering whimper made me turn my head. A mistake, as my vision swam again. When it cleared, I was staring into the wide, dilated eyes of the wolf, half-hidden behind a broken cart a few feet away from me, and cowering like a guilty hunting dog expecting to be whipped by its master. Its muzzle was coated with dried gore from the fallen soldier lying in a heap across from us.

Shouting and hoof beats echoed along the central roadway, and the animal flattened itself even further against the ground, obviously terrified. I rolled painfully over to lie on my back on the packed dirt, craning my neck until I got an upside-down view of Volya's returning party. Andoc was at the front. He reined his galloping horse to an abrupt halt even as the others rode past, heading further into the village where the destruction was greatest.

Easy on that poor gelding's mouth, I thought as Andoc jumped down and raced toward me, his worried expression looking almost comical upside down. He skidded to a stop midway between my body and that of the wolf, looking back and forth between us as if torn. A moment later, he was kneeling at my side, lifting me to cradle my shoulders carefully in his arms. I smiled up at his warm, brown eyes, feeling giddy.

"Careful, there's a man-eating wolf here," I said, and promptly slipped back into unconsciousness.

The next time I awoke, I was inside a hut, lying on a straw mattress on the floor. I stared up at the golden brown thatch visible through the rafters overhead for several moments, blinking. A snug bandage circled my forehead, and I could feel the cool stickiness from some sort of poultice pressed against my throbbing temple. My vision seemed steadier, and the earth was no longer moving in stately, ponderous circles beneath me.

I wasn't alone. I could hear the sound of retching followed by ragged, unsteady breathing from across the room. Someone else was whispering a litany of soothing reassurance. I rolled gingerly onto my side, lifting my aching head with considerable effort and propping myself on one elbow so I could see. Seated on a wide, low bed frame against the far wall, Senovo was slumped sideways with his forehead resting against Andoc's shoulder, breathing heavily. Andoc's hand cradled the back of his neck, steadying him, and a chamber pot rested on the ground in front of him. The priest was naked from the waist up, a blanket thrown carelessly over his lap. His face was canted toward me. I could see dried blood coating his jaw and neck, along with a livid bruise above his left eyebrow. His eyes were tightly closed as he struggled for composure.

There was something… something about the blood and the bruise… but no. My wits were still too addled to make whatever connection it was that dangled tantalizingly just out of reach. Andoc turned slightly, and his eyes met mine. His fingers tightened around the back of the distraught priest's head for a moment, then relaxed.

"Senovo," he said softly, "she's awake."

THREE

My blood ran cold at the three simple words, even as Senovo opened anguished eyes, straightening away from his friend's support. I was suddenly, painfully aware that, like Senovo, I was naked under the rough blanket covering me.

Oh, gods. They knew. They knew my secret.

Something of my horror must have shown on my face, because Andoc raised a hand, as one might do when faced with a wild, unpredictable animal.

"I apologize," he said. "You were unconscious and there was blood soaking your breeches. I thought you'd been wounded in an exceptionally unfortunate place. I had no way of knowing it was moon blood."

"You had no right!" I said, struggling upright on the straw-stuffed palliasse with the blanket clutched around me.

Andoc raised his eyebrows. "Well, I suppose next time I'll know to leave you bleeding in the street, in that case. Live and learn." The hint of humor in his voice set my blood boiling.

"You could at least have kept it to yourself instead of spilling my secret to the very next person you saw," I snapped. "Now both of you know!"

"I knew already, Carivel," Senovo said, sounding exhausted but looking somewhat more composed than before. Andoc's attention immediately returned to the priest. He dipped a rag in the bowl of water resting on the table next to the bed, and started wiping at the blood on Senovo's face with a sure touch.

"How could you know?" I asked derisively. "No one knew!"

"The wolf smelled the blood on you earlier," said Senovo, gently moving Andoc's hand away and taking the rag to finish cleaning off his face himself.

"The... wolf?" I asked stupidly. The wolf that I had bruised over one eye with a rock. Just like the bruise now darkening Senovo's face. The wolf that tore out a man's throat, getting blood all over its mouth and jaw. Saving my life.

"Consider it an exchange," Senovo said. "A secret for a secret."

"You're a shape-shifter?" I asked, completely taken aback. People who could transform themselves into animals were incredibly rare, and almost always rose quickly through the ranks of the priesthood to become powerful religious figures. "But... you're a priest. Why keep such a power secret?"

"Because I can't control it. Because it makes me a killer."

"Bullshit," Andoc said matter-of-factly. "*I'm* a killer. You're a mild-mannered religious man who happens to turn into a wolf sometimes."

Senovo's brows drew together, a furrow of anger forming between them. "I think there's at least one man lying in the street with his throat ripped out who would beg to differ with you… if he weren't *already dead*."

"Pfft. He was an enemy soldier. I'd've killed him myself, if I'd been here," said Andoc in a dismissive tone.

"You aren't a priest," Senovo replied.

"I imagine Carivel here is plenty relieved that he's dead, by a priest's hand or not," Andoc countered.

"Yes and no," I said cautiously, looking between the two of them. "I'm not dead, but my life here may be as good as over, regardless. Does anybody else know? About me, I mean?"

"Not as far as I'm aware," Senovo said.

Andoc shrugged. "I certainly haven't told anyone. Who you choose to be makes no difference to me."

"Well, it makes a very big difference to me!" I flared. "The horses are my life, and women aren't allowed to work with them! Speaking of which, if I ever see you yank on your gelding's mouth again like you did this morning, I'll have Jorun confiscate your bridle and make you use a hackamore until you learn to ride properly!"

Shouting at him felt good. I resolved to do it more often. Too bad the only effect it had was to make his lips quirk as if he were holding back a smile.

"I'll keep it in mind," he said. "As for the other thing — the gods and religious law and such — that's more Senovo's area than mine."

Almost against my will, my eyes moved back to the young priest, expecting to see some form of censure for my years of heresy.

"Yes, it's all terribly shocking," he said, sounding tired but not, in point of fact, terribly shocked. "Really, it's amazing that your female presence hasn't decimated the herd over the past few years since you arrived. How odd that it is, in fact, thriving under your care—larger and of better quality than it has ever been. It's utterly inexplicable."

It was obvious that I was being teased.

"You're not a very good priest," I said, my eyes narrowed in anger.

"I know," Senovo agreed readily. "Not only am I a killer, I also question the gods' wisdom when it doesn't make logical sense. High priest Rhystel would be appalled if he found out I'd been blessed with the power to shift."

"I still say you should tell him sometime, just to see the look on his face," Andoc said.

"So, basically," I said, trying to get the conversation back on track, "if I don't tell anyone you're a shifter, you and Andoc won't tell anyone that I was born female?"

"If you want to look at it that way," Senovo said, not unkindly. "In fact, I have more sympathy and understanding than you might suspect for the disharmony between how one perceives oneself and what is hanging—or not hanging—between one's legs."

"And, as I said earlier," Andoc added, "I don't particularly care if you've got a prick or a cunt. I rather like you, regardless. You've got courage. I respect that."

Senovo sighed. "You've missed your calling as a poet, my friend. You have *such* a way with words."

Could it really be that simple? Agree to keep each other's secrets, and go on as if nothing had happened?

"You have nothing to fear from me, Senovo," I said cautiously. "If we're agreed that neither of these revelations ever took place, then I'm in your debt. You saved my life last night."

"I'm glad something good came of it, in that case," Senovo said.

"Sorry about the rock," I added, gesturing to his bruised face.

"Don't mention it," he said, and Andoc snorted.

I suddenly realized that in my horror at being discovered, I'd completely forgotten to ask about the battle. "What... happened, exactly, last night? After I lost consciousness, I mean."

The way Andoc's face went abruptly grim and angry made my heart sink in my chest. I looked to Senovo, who shook his head.

"I only shifted back a few minutes before you woke up," he said.

"I didn't want to leave you two alone for long, so I don't know details yet," Andoc said. "It's not good, though. If you're both well enough, we should probably go help outside."

Senovo nodded agreement, and gave his face a final scrub with the rag. Andoc looked at me questioningly.

"Where are my clothes?" I asked.

"On the stool," he said, indicating the rough wooden seat near the mattress where I was sitting.

Senovo stood, unbothered by his own nakedness as he reached for the robes Andoc handed him and shrugged them on. I tried not to stare, feeling a blush crawl up my face, which deepened further when I caught Andoc watching me. The two of them left the hut to give me privacy, and I dressed as quickly as I could. My breeches were still stiff with the rusty stain of dried moon blood, but in the aftermath of a battle no one would question it. I had to pause occasionally to regain my balance as my injured head swam, but I became steadier the more I moved around. The headache was phenomenal, however.

Andoc's hut was close to the north edge of the village, and when I exited the sturdy structure, things didn't seem too bad at first. Andoc and Senovo were waiting for me outside, and Andoc led the way toward the center of the settlement, where I had tried to take on armed soldiers with a horsewhip earlier. I shivered slightly. By all rights, I should be dead.

The smell of stale smoke grew more noticeable the further we went. When we turned a corner into the village green that served as a central meeting place, I stumbled to a halt, my breath catching in my throat. People were carrying bodies onto the green, laying them out in neat rows. Bodies that I *recognized.*

How utterly, utterly stupid of me not to have understood until now that people *I knew* had been killed. I thought back to the flames — to the chaos and the screaming. Of course people had died. Of *course* they had. I suddenly felt ill, and very, very young.

A hand grasped my upper arm in a steadying grip.

"Come," said Senovo, still looking pale though his voice had regained its usual even timbre. "Let us go see what we can do to help."

I nodded, a feeling of numbness washing over me. Andoc had already attracted Volya's attention and was speaking to him as we approached.

"How many dead?" Andoc asked.

"They've found two dozen so far," Volya replied, looking as if he'd aged twenty years overnight. "There are still several houses and other buildings that need to be searched, though." The chief looked to Senovo, and I felt the priest's hand tighten reflexively on my arm for an instant before he deliberately removed it. "Senovo, I'm sorry to be the bearer of bad news. They attacked the priests and acolytes in the temple barracks."

Beside me, Senovo sucked in an audible breath. Andoc looked at him with worried eyes.

"High Priest Rhystel?" Senovo asked, and I could hear the strain behind the carefully level voice.

"Gravely injured," Volya said. The anger that had been lurking behind the old chief's expression came to the forefront. "They left him for dead. Healer Sagdea is with him."

"I should go to him," Senovo said, sounding distant. He blinked, recalling himself to the present conversation. "And… the others in the barracks?"

"All killed, except for two of the younger acolytes," Volya said. "Raston hid in a storage chest during the attack, and Crenelo was visiting a friend elsewhere in the village. Those vicious Alyrion bastards think they can break us by attacking our religion. If they had their way, we'd all be worshipping their thrice-damned deity. Damick, or Damock, or whatever it is they call it."

Senovo nodded his understanding, that same look of distance returning to his eyes. I was debating internally whether to steady him with a hand on his arm as he had done for me when Volya addressed me directly.

"Carivel. Dalon reports that all of the horses are gone. I think we have to assume that they were stolen by the invaders," he said.

"No!" I said quickly, shaking my head. "No, I was watching your mare last night when I heard the fighting. Once I saw what was going on, I let the horses out of the pens and drove them toward the summer pastures and the foothills."

Volya looked surprised, but pleased. "Is that so? That's the first piece of good news I've heard today. Well done, lad. That was quick thinking."

"It was nothing," I said, uncomfortable with the praise in the midst of such terrible circumstances. "We'll have to go round them up again as soon as possible, though, and it's a large area to search. Where is Jorun?"

"I haven't seen him," Volya said.

A wave of worry washed over me. I was surprised that it had been Dalon and not the Horse Master himself who found the horses missing. Hopefully the old man hadn't been injured during the battle.

My thoughts were interrupted by a cry of grief from across the green. All four of us turned to see three of Gretya's daughters clinging to each other, huddled around the door to Jorun's sleeping hut. My heart sank.

We hurried across to the little house with its crooked doorframe and cheerful boxes of herbs hanging under the windows. The wail had come from Limdya, who was now weeping loudly into her older sister's shoulder. Volya murmured quietly to the girls, urging them away from the door so that Andoc, Senovo and I could enter.

Blood painted the walls of the small structure in ugly splashes, and I had to breathe deeply as my head started to spin again. Gretya's twisted form lay motionless on the bed, her lifeblood staining her linen nightshirt a dull brown around the wound that had pierced her heart. My gaze skittered away from the pitiful sight of the old woman's body, coming to rest instead on the second figure lying on the floor with a short sword still clasped in one gnarled hand.

FOUR

A pained, animal noise escaped my throat as I recognized Jorun, his familiar face frozen in a grimace of pain and fear. Behind me, I heard Volya groan in dismay.

I was right about him and Gretya, I thought, even as I struggled to draw breath. Jorun's eyes were open, staring at a point over my left shoulder. I found that I was backing away through the door unsteadily, my legs threatening to buckle beneath me and send me sprawling on the ground. More of the pained noises were emerging from my lips with each strangled breath—I couldn't seem to stop them.

Hands closed around my arms from either side, supporting me as I continued to stagger backwards, away from the terrible sight.

"That's right. Come away," Andoc said from my right shoulder.

"Deep breaths," Senovo said from my left. "Focus on us."

I tried, I really did—gasping for air that seemed too thick and stale with smoke from burned huts and burned bodies. I was vaguely aware of the sound of the three newly orphaned sisters weeping a short distance away. Andoc was in front of me now, taking my face in his hands as Senovo kept me upright.

"Breathe now," Andoc said, forcing me to meet his gaze eye-to-eye. "We will grieve later. You have people relying on you. Carivel, you are the Horse Master now, and Draebard's horses are running loose in the foothills."

I stared at him like some kind of simpleton. I was the *what*? Oh, gods. The old Horse Master was dead, and I was the Horse Master's assistant. I felt a jolt through my chest like I'd been kicked by a fractious yearling, and air flooded my lungs at last as I sucked in a gasping breath, and another, and another. The fog in my mind cleared slightly, and I tried to focus on the throbbing of the bruise on my temple — grasping at the dull pain like a lifeline.

"That's it," Andoc said encouragingly, as Senovo cautiously released his grip and left me to stand unaided.

"But... Jorun," I said, my eyes drifting over Andoc's shoulder and toward the crooked doorway. "I should... "

"Volya and I will take care of Jorun and Gretya," Andoc said, pulling my focus back to him. "You should go find Dalon and whoever else you need to round up the horses. Senovo, go to the temple and see if the healer needs any help with Rhystel."

I nodded, my face still framed within Andoc's callused hands, feeling the odd numbness from earlier returning. That same numbness kept me from reacting when Andoc pressed his lips briefly to my bandaged forehead before letting me go. My eyes sought Senovo, who dipped his chin in acknowledgement, his own face pale and haggard as he turned to leave for the temple barracks.

I felt strangely detached from events as I turned to Volya, who had stepped back to give the three of us some privacy.

"I will need use of the horses you and your party were riding," I said.

He nodded. "Leave one in case we have to get a message out for some reason. The rest are at your disposal."

I took my leave, barely able to feel my boots against the ground as my feet carried me toward the horse pens without any conscious direction on my part. Thinking about the details of what I would need to recapture the herd was good. It gave me something to focus on, forcing my mind into working again like a rusty wheel on a chariot axle. My own gelding, Kekenu, was loose with the herd. If I could get within whistling distance, he would come to my call, and we could let him lead us back to the others.

By the time I reached the pens, I had the bare outline of a plan. Between the wolf and the battle, the horses had been in a panic last night. They would probably have headed for the perceived safety of the foothills rather than staying in the open pastureland, though they'd likely ventured down to graze today, now that things were quiet. We would look in the valleys at the base of the hills, and work our way out from there if necessary.

Dalon and several of the other boys were clustered around the pens. Some of the younger ones were obviously fighting tears. I would have to lead them. I would have to do for them what Jorun had always done for us, before.

"Come here, all of you," I said loudly as I approached. The lads looked up in surprise, and I continued as they grudgingly gathered around. "The horses are loose somewhere in the vicinity of the foothills. We need to go get them."

"Why do you think they're in the foothills?" Dalon asked in open challenge. "I reckon the soldiers stole 'em all during the raid."

"I know they're in the foothills because I'm the one who let them out of the pens and drove them in that direction last night, so the soldiers couldn't get them," I said, and a murmur went around the group. "Now, we need to get them back before they wander too far."

"Where's Jorun?" asked a young boy named Favian.

My stomach churned, and it was as if I was listening to someone else speaking as I answered, "Jorun is dead."

There were several gasps and cries of denial. Favian burst into tears, and his friend Lundis put an awkward arm around him. Jorun had been like a father to many of these boys. I allowed the expressions of shock and grief to continue for several seconds before speaking up again.

"Jorun died bravely, with a sword in his hand," I said eventually, raising my voice enough to be heard. "We owe it to him to do our jobs and make him proud. Draebard's strength lies with its warriors and its horses. Our warriors drove off a cowardly and dishonorable attack last night, saving the village from complete destruction. It's up to us to get back our horses so those same warriors can descend on our new enemy with a swarm of battle chariots and destroy them utterly."

The boys were all quiet now—looking at me. Looking *to* me, though Dalon and a few others wore sour expressions. I wondered with an odd sort of detached panic how I was ever going to live up to Jorun's memory.

"Now," I said, "get all of the horses from Volya's riding party saddled except for the gray mare with the scar on her shoulder. We'll head out as soon as we can. Favian, I want you and Lundis to stay here in case Chief Volya needs to send out a message. Favian will ready the pens with feed and water for our return, and Lundis, you will check in periodically with Volya in case he needs you to act as a courier."

There was a split second of silence—just long enough for panic to thread through the pall of numbness hanging over me and start crawling up my spine—but then the little crowd broke up and started to carry out my instructions. Releasing a quiet breath of relief, I went to gather extra ropes, halters, and whips, along with a pocketful of dried apples.

Half an hour later, ten of us rode out along the track leading north away from the village. The chaotic hoof prints left by the herd's headlong flight were still visible on the dusty road beneath us. The foothills were more than an hour away on horseback, and our little group was largely silent at first. As our horses' hooves ate up the distance, though, Dalon could no longer contain his disagreement with my plan.

"We should have started searching close to the village and worked our way out. There's no reason to start looking so far away," he said, pitching his voice for those riding closest to him. Fortunately—or perhaps unfortunately—my hearing was excellent.

"The horses were panicked by the commotion and the smell of burning," I said evenly. "They will have sought shelter and safety in the hills."

"Maybe they did and maybe they didn't," Dalon said. "I guess we'll find out, won't we?"

It was already midday. If I was wrong and the horses were far away from the hills somewhere, we would lose the light before we could find them. It would have been all too easy to start second-guessing myself, which was exactly what Dalon wanted, I suspected. The fact remained though—I knew horses. After I fled the village of my birth and my mother's bitter anger over what she saw as my failings, I wandered the wildlands for weeks, tracking herds of native Eburosi ponies for days at a time to learn about their behavior. I had been drawn to horses my whole life—their strength, their speed and power. When I could no longer trust myself to endure the vicious words and even more vicious beatings doled out by the woman who'd given birth to me, I decided to flee my home and find out for myself if someone with the body of a woman could control the spirits of horses.

I succeeded, and it was that success which gave me the idea to start somewhere new, living as a man. My own little black and white gelding came from one of those wildland herds I'd followed. Working on foot, I had tamed him away from his herd-mates as a yearling after he'd been weakened by an ugly leg injury. Gaining his trust had taken nearly a week and was one of my proudest accomplishments, second only to attaining my position as Jorun's assistant. Thinking of Jorun made my chest start aching, so I tore my mind away from that train of thought. The point was, I knew horses. And I knew that Draebard's herd would be close to the foothills.

"Spread out," I called as we finally approached the gently sloping valleys south of the hills. "Stay within shouting distance of each other and call out if you see anything."

Clouds were moving in from the southwest, blocking out the afternoon sun. It would rain before the evening was over. I eased Andoc's gelding away from the others, silently cursing the animal's hard mouth, along with Andoc's hard hands that had made it that way. The bay gelding shook his head in annoyance, but eventually peeled away from his herd mates obediently. Keeping to the ridge tops, I stood in the stirrups, craning around to scan the waves of green grass swept by the wind.

Every few minutes, I let out a shrill whistle, in hopes that Kekenu was within hearing distance. The other boys shouted reports back and forth as they searched. For almost two hours we continued in that manner, the lads growing progressively more impatient and sullen. A brisk wind blew a handful of spattered raindrops against my face just as I heard the distant hoof beats of a single horse approaching.

FIVE

I wet my dry lips and whistled again.

A moment later, Kekenu came charging into sight, his pinto coat a bright contrast against the green grass.

"Kekenu is here! They must be close!" I shouted to the nearest boy, before dismounting and leading Andoc's horse forward to meet the little gelding.

Kekenu bounded to a stop a few feet away from me, snorting and tossing his head. When he calmed, I motioned him forward the last few steps and fed him a piece of dried apple. By this time, several of the lads had converged on us.

"Here," I said, handing Andoc's horse off to one of them. "Take Andoc's gelding. We'll let Kekenu lead us back to the rest of the herd."

I grabbed a length of thin rope from my saddlebag and tied it in a loop around the base of Kekenu's neck—since I was letting the little horse choose his own path, I didn't need anything fancier than a simple neck rope for control. Facing his flank and grabbing a hank of mane in my left hand, I bounded forward a step and vaulted up onto his low back, scooting my hips sideways with a little jerk to center myself. A quick head count showed that all of the others had joined us.

"Follow me!" I called, and urged Kekenu into motion with a squeeze of my calves.

The little horse surged forward eagerly, one ear flicked back until it became obvious that I did not have a destination in mind. He cantered around in a broad arc until we were headed back in the direction he'd come from, the others keeping pace behind us. The horse's muscles bunched and released rhythmically between my thighs as I balanced on his broad, familiar back, one hand still wrapped in the gelding's generous mane. The rain was coming down more steadily now.

After only a few minutes, we crested a small hill and there, laid out below us, was the herd. I breathed a sigh of relief. The horses—nearly a hundred of them—looked up at the disturbance as we approached. My eyes scanned them eagerly. They were moving around too much to get a proper head count, but my attention was drawn to a creamy white yearling. Cassira—the pale colt's dam—was standing nearby, keeping watch over a small, white bundle on the ground. The tiny creature stirred from its slumber and stumbled awkwardly to its feet on long, uncoordinated legs, shaking its little head in consternation before making straight for its mother's udder and drinking greedily. Another tiny piece of the tension curled inside me eased at the sight.

"Volya's mare foaled sometime earlier today," I called, pointing down at the spindly white figure. "We'll have to take it slowly on the way back. Everyone, skirt around to the north and let's drive them on to Draebard. Nice and easy, mind."

The boys ranged around the herd, giving the nervous animals a wide berth. I nodded in satisfaction as Dalon and Tenibral eased up to the front, leading the way. Both were mounted on mares that were relatively high in the herd's pecking order, and when the rest of us started putting pressure on the horses from behind, they easily followed the two mares' lead without panicking and running. I settled myself near the back, where I could watch for stragglers and keep an eye on the newborn foal trotting easily next to Cassira on its gangly legs.

The rain increased to a steady patter—not a downpour, but enough to soak through clothing and run down the backs of our necks in a chilly, unpleasant trickle. It took nearly twice as long to get back as it had to go out, and tempers were short by the time we finally reached the familiar track leading to the pens. The sky was fading from slate gray to black when the last horse trotted through the gate, eager to get to the feed Favian had laid out for them. We unsaddled the riding horses quickly and turned them loose as well.

I wavered for a moment before deciding to separate Cassira and her new foal from the others. No doubt the foal would be fine with the herd it had been born into earlier in the day, but in the small pen with the run-in shed, the pair could get out of the chilly spring rain and sleep somewhere dry.

Cassira pinned her ears and charged at me when I approached with the halter, only to come to a surprised halt as the end of the lead rope snapped stingingly across her chest.

"Yes, you're a very fierce mama," I told her, "but it's getting late, and I'm tired and cold. Now hush and come here."

The horse flung her head up and down twice, subsiding as I approached and fed her a piece of the now rather damp and spongy dried apple from my pocket. I slipped the halter on and, with a glance to ensure the foal was following, led the pair into the second pen where a pile of hay was waiting in the shed. Upon her release, Cassira went straight for her feed. I relaxed against the wall under the overhang, staying completely still as the tiny, pale foal approached and began to sniff at my wet clothing and skin.

I was losing the light, but I stayed there for a little while anyway. Eventually the young horse gained enough confidence to let me run my hands over its shoulder and back, scratching lightly until I found an itchy place that had it twisting its little head and neck into funny contortions with ecstasy. Its white coat seemed to glow with a faint, ghostly light in the encroaching darkness.

The boys had finished putting everything away and readying the pens for nighttime when I left and closed the gate behind me. They were gathered under the eaves of the storage building, talking quietly when I approached.

"Well done, all of you," I told them. "This has been a terrible day for Draebard, but each of you has done Jorun proud. Go dry off and get something to eat. Try to get some rest and I'll see you back here in the morning."

When everyone had dispersed, muttering unenthusiastically as they went, I let myself slump back against the rough wooden wall. The events of the day seemed to crash over me like a wave, leaving me exhausted and making the pounding in my already sore head even worse. A shiver wracked me, and I realized with sudden clarity that I was freezing beneath my wet clothing in the evening chill.

I knew I wouldn't feel right leaving the horses unguarded tonight, but it would be safe enough to return to my tiny hut at the edge of town for a few minutes to get some dry clothing and a rain cloak. Forcing myself upright, I trudged through the cold rain along the muddy road until my familiar door loomed out of the dark. I paused a few steps from the entrance in surprise. Candlelight was shining through the single small window.

"Who's there?" I snapped, yanking open the door.

Inside, Andoc looked up at me mildly from where he'd been lounging on the edge of my bed, eating a hunk of flatbread spread with soft cheese.

"Sorry," he said around a mouthful, pausing to swallow before he continued. "When I saw the rest of Jorun's boys were back, I thought you might want something to eat. Brought you that."

He indicated the rest of the bread and cheese with a jerk of his chin, the simple repast sitting on my rickety little table.

"Oh," I said, at a loss for anything more intelligent. "Thanks."

"You staying with the horses tonight?" he asked, taking another large bite.

"Yes," I said, and set myself to spreading cheese on my own portion of bread. "Where's Senovo?"

"Still with the high priest. Reston and Crenelo are there, as well. The poor boys are distraught, as you might imagine."

Tears threatened to rise up and choke me. I fought them down with a harsh swallow.

"How is Rhystel?" I made myself ask.

Andoc shrugged. "His wounds are serious, and he's an old man. It's not good."

"How many died, altogether?" I asked, not at all sure I wanted the answer.

"Thirty-eight, that we've been able to find," Andoc said. "Another twenty-three badly injured."

"Gods," I said faintly.

"The remaining elders are meeting in the morning to discuss our retaliation," Andoc said. "I assume you got all the horses back safe?"

"Yes," I replied. "Tell Volya that he has his white foal, if you get a chance. It seems strong and healthy. I don't know yet if it's a colt or filly."

"He'll be glad to hear that, at least."

I nodded, finishing the slab of bread. Another shiver wracked me.

"You're soaked," Andoc said with a frown. "You should change clothes and warm up before you go back. Do you want me to leave?"

"Please," I whispered, numb from more than the cold.

Andoc nodded and left, laying a hand on my shoulder briefly as he did so. I stripped out of my wet clothing and ran a threadbare towel over my body before donning a spare set of buckskin trousers and a tunic. Distantly, I noted that my moon bleeding seemed to have finally stopped. After donning a tattered rain cloak, I returned to the horse pens and curled up on a pile of hay in the storage building, where I would hear any disturbance coming from outside.

Burying my head in my arms, I let the tears come.

⛊

The following morning dawned gray and chill, but at least the rain had stopped during the night. My headache was duller, though still very much present. My eyes were red and swollen. With a sigh, I unwrapped the dirty bandage from my head, using the stained linen to gingerly brush off the remaining poultice, which had dried into a flaky mess over the bruise on my temple. The boys would be here soon, and I probably looked like a pile of two-day-old manure at this point.

Dragging myself outside, I walked straight to the nearest horse trough and dunked my head in the cold water, scrubbing at my face and hair until I couldn't hold my breath any longer. When I emerged, I didn't feel *better*, exactly… but I did feel more awake. The lads began to trickle in a few minutes later, most of them looking like they'd had nights not much better than my own. Dalon and two of his mates were the last to arrive.

"We need to check the horses for injuries this morning," I told them when everyone had assembled. "The herd was in a full blown stampede when I drove them off. It's likely there are some cuts and bruises."

"I still say you're not automatically the one in charge, like you seem to think you are," Dalon said from the back.

"Carivel was right about the horses being in the foothills, though, wasn't he?" young Favian piped up before I could think of a suitable response. "If we'd followed what you said, we wouldn't have got the horses back before dark yesterday."

"An' he was Jorun's assistant, everyone knows that," Lundis added. "Who else would be in charge now?"

I put up a hand to quiet them. "Regardless of who's in charge, we all know what needs to be done," I said. "The horses need to be checked over and taken out to the spring pastures—under supervision, this time. The pens need mucking out, and we need to haul the manure to the vegetable plots for fertilizer. Dalon, are we at least agreed on that?"

"'Course," Dalon said. "Everyone here knows that."

"Then it hardly matters who says it," I said. "So, we'll all go through and check for injuries. Who was slated to take the herd out today?"

"Me, Kerney, and Lundis," said Varin, one of Dalon's hangers-on.

"Fine. The rest of us will clean the pens and take a break at lunchtime," I said.

There was a bit of muttering, but no one argued. We moved through the herd, smearing salve on scrapes and cuts; checking for heat in swollen limbs. All told, the horses had fared well during their brief, unplanned foray into the wilderness. While the lads in charge of taking the horses out to graze readied their mounts, I beckoned to Favian. The boy was one of the youngest here, but he already showed a great deal of promise with the animals. When he reached me, I gestured to the pen where Cassira and the white foal were lazing in the corner.

"Come with me, Favian," I said. "We need to check the foal and work on getting it tame."

I was pleased to see his pale face light up for the first time since the attack at the prospect of getting to work with the valuable white foal. I handed him a length of soft rope and reminded him to keep an eye on the mare as we entered. The young horse was nursing when we approached. Cassira pinned her ears and pawed with one front foot, but did not move otherwise.

"Colt or filly?" I asked Favian, who worked his way around until he could get a peek under the foal's flapping tail.

"It's a colt!" he said. "Just like last year's!"

"Volya will be pleased," I said. "Looks like he's got his white chariot team after all."

Under my watchful eye, Favian approached Cassira's head and scratched it until she stopped fussing. When the mare was relaxed, he moved back to run his hands over the oblivious foal's haunches as it nursed. I directed him to stroke down the colt's legs and lift them one at a time while it continued its single-minded pursuit of milk, accustoming the youngster to having its feet handled.

When the colt's stomach was full, it craned around, startling in place comically as it truly noticed Favian for the first time. Before long, though, the boy found the same itchy spot I'd discovered last night and scratched it, sending the foal into paroxysms of pleasure.

"That's enough for this morning," I said when the little horse seemed in danger of tipping over in its attempts to lean harder against the scratching fingers. "Always leave them wanting more, Favian."

Favian grinned over at me, yesterday's trauma momentarily banished in the joy of befriending the young animal. I clapped him companionably on the shoulder as he rejoined me. The two of us left the pen to join the others, grabbing shovels and pushcarts along the way. Meanwhile, Varin, Kerney, and Lundis herded most of the rest of the horses out to graze, leaving a few behind in case anyone in the village needed transportation.

The familiar routine of cleaning the pens was soothing, and the morning passed quietly enough. It was nearing lunchtime when a boy from the village ran up, calling for me.

"I'm here," I answered, putting my shovel aside.

The child only came up to my waist, but he puffed up self-importantly as he delivered his message. "Chief Volya requests your presence in the meeting house right away, Horse Master Carivel!"

My first reaction at being addressed in such a way was shock, but I'll admit I was not above feeling a twinge of satisfaction at seeing Dalon's discomfiture. I could practically feel the disgust radiating from him.

"I'll be there momentarily," I told the boy. After a second's thought, I caught Dalon's eye. "Would you mind organizing the lads when they get back from lunch? I'm not sure what the chief needs me for, or how long I'll be."

Dalon watched me warily, but he merely said. "Yeah, all right. I'll set them to cleaning the saddles and bridles from yesterday. They need tallow rubbed on them after being in the rain."

"Good idea," I said. "Thank you."

He stared at me for a few more seconds, but didn't add anything else as I turned and headed toward the village meeting hall.

When I arrived, it appeared that the meeting was breaking up. People were leaving, but as I stuck my head inside, Andoc immediately noticed me and waved me over to where he was speaking with Volya.

"Carivel," Volya greeted. "Thank you for coming so quickly—I'm sure you must be busy. I have a task for you. I'm sending Andoc and Senovo to talk with the Mereni, in hopes of gaining their military support against those spineless Alyrion bastards who attacked us."

I blinked. That *was* an interesting bit of news. People in Draebard looked down on the Mereni to the extent that they would barely even talk about them or acknowledge their existence. But what did a potential alliance with our neighbors to the east have to do with me?

"Andoc suggested that you go with them," Volya continued. "The Mereni respect good horse trainers, and he seems to think you would be uniquely suited to dealing with them."

What?

Andoc was looking at me, one eyebrow raised slightly as if in challenge, and I felt the sudden irrational urge to wipe that cocky expression off his face with my fist. My mouth was open. I closed it, and swallowed twice.

"If you think I would be of help, I'm happy to do whatever I can," I managed.

"Good lad," said Volya. "The Mereni village is two days' ride. You'll leave in the morning. This evening, we will be holding a funeral ceremony for those who died."

Suddenly, the grief hit me afresh, like a sharp blow to the sternum, and it was all I could do to nod and say, "Of course." Volya clapped a hand on my shoulder and excused himself, leaving me alone with Andoc and my churning emotions.

"Why?" I asked cautiously, looking up at him.

His smug expression had faded at the mention of the funeral ceremony. "The Mereni really do have respect for horse tamers and trainers," he said. "As for the rest, well, you'll understand when we get there. Now, have you eaten at all since I brought you food last night?"

It took a few moments more than it should have to think back. "No," I said eventually.

"My surprise knows no bounds." Apparently, neither did his sarcasm. I frowned as he continued. "Very well, you're coming with me to deliver lunch to Senovo and help make sure he eats it. Let's go."

It had taken no time at all for Gretya's daughters to throw themselves into taking over her business with the single-mindedness of people who were trying to keep grief at bay. I watched in something of a daze as Andoc charmed an extra portion from the girls, and I returned the teary hug that Limdya offered me, patting her somewhat awkwardly on the back. Andoc and I made our way to the temple barracks, laden with fruit, cheese, and cold meat. While I was familiar with the building's location, I'd never really had cause to spend much time there. It was the largest structure in the settlement, decorated with carved stone and beaten metal representing the various deities.

Andoc stopped at the door, offering a perfunctory obeisance to the gods, and I followed suit. Inside, it seemed far too quiet and empty. An effort had been made to clean up the damage and, presumably, the blood. All of the priests' bodies had been removed to the green with the others, but the building still seemed more like a crypt than a place where people lived. I shivered, unable to help myself. Toward the end of the long, narrow structure, we heard the faint sound of voices and followed them. Andoc cleared his throat as we approached, and Senovo looked up from the chair he was occupying next to High Priest Rhystel's low pallet.

"Greetings," Andoc said, "We come bearing food, and news."

"Ah," said the High Priest in a weak voice, "Andoc. Perhaps you can convince young Senovo here to stop hovering for an hour or two and go get some rest. Oh, hello, Carivel."

"Hello," I said, trying to smile and failing miserably.

"I've given up trying to get the stubborn bastard to do anything he doesn't want to, Elder Brother. Perhaps between us, we can at least get these two to eat, though," Andoc said, shocking me a bit with his informality. *Elder Brother* and *Little Brother* were terms the priests used with each other, based on their comparative rank. I had never heard someone outside of the priesthood address any of them in such a way, much less the High Priest.

The old man huffed a soft breath of pained laughter. "Indeed, my boy. Indeed."

Rhystel was deathly pale. His upper body was swathed with bandages, soaked through with blood under his right shoulder. One of the invading soldiers must have run him through and left him, thinking him dead. The blood loss itself was bad enough for someone of the High Priest's advanced years, but if infection set in it would all be over very quickly.

54

Andoc set his burden of food on a low table nearby, and motioned me to do the same. "Eat," he said firmly. I picked up a slice of meat without argument and started eating. Andoc spread another slice with cheese, rolled it up, and handed it to Senovo, who had remained silent throughout.

"Are you able to eat anything, Elder Brother?" Andoc asked.

"That depends. Are those fresh lindanberries I smell?" Rhystel asked.

"They are," Andoc replied, and gathered a small handful.

"The healer said you were only to have broth," Senovo said, his voice rusty as if he had not used it for a while.

Rhystel smiled up at him kindly. "If this is to be my last season on earth, I would like to enjoy the lindanberries while I have a chance, Little Brother."

Senovo subsided, but his expression was distraught. I ached for him, and for the loss of my own mentor.

"And what brings you here, Carivel?" Rhystel asked.

I forced myself to meet his eyes, trying once again to smile. "I seem to be acting as a pack horse for the most part, High Priest. Though, speaking of horses, you might be interested to know that Volya's mare foaled a second white colt yesterday."

"Ah, that's a good omen," said the old man, pausing to let Andoc feed him a berry.

"Senovo," Andoc said, "you, Carivel, and I are to ride out to the Mereni village tomorrow morning. Volya wants to forge an alliance with them against the troops at the Alyrion outpost."

"Really?" Senovo said with a faint frown, showing the first stirrings of interest. "The Mereni? That's… unusual."

"Well, well," the High Priest said. "Extraordinary times call for extraordinary measures, I suppose. Now, if the three of you are finished eating, please go away for a while and let an old eunuch get some rest. Senovo, you have a ceremony to prepare for, I believe."

I suddenly realized that Senovo would, by necessity, be performing the funeral rites this evening. It seemed his desire to remain a figure lurking in the background was not destined to be. He looked as though the very thought made him nauseous, but he allowed Andoc to usher him away nonetheless. I set myself to tidying away the remains of the food.

"Shall I leave these for you, High Priest?" I asked, indicating the small bowl of berries.

"Please," he said, and I set them next to him, within easy reach of his good arm. "Carivel," he continued, his eyes closing and his voice sounding suddenly far away, "this is important. Don't be afraid to seize opportunity when it comes your way. The gods place doors in front of us; it is up to us to walk through them."

I stilled, trying to make sense of his words. "Thank you, High Priest Rhystel," I said eventually. "I'll try to remember."

Distracted, I left Andoc trying to get Senovo to rest, and returned to the pens. It was not yet midafternoon, so I busied myself with the others, oiling leather that had gotten wet in the rain the previous day to prevent it from stiffening and cracking. When the boys tending the herd drove them back to the pens at dinnertime, I gathered everyone to inform them of the funeral, and my impending absence.

"Dalon," I said, "you will be in charge while I'm gone. Favian, you will assist him. I would also like you to continue taming Cassira's foal, Favian."

Dalon appeared stuck between irritation and smug pride; Favian looked surprised, but pleased. I dismissed everyone to go about their business, and returned to my hut in hopes of girding myself for the funeral ceremony in a couple of hours.

SIX

The entire village turned out at dusk, gathering on the village green. A pyre had been laid at some point during the day. I had to suppress a shudder at the sight of the bodies wrapped in shrouds and resting on the pile of stacked wood; I'd never seen a funeral fire so large, and I never wanted to again. I had intended to find a place near the back, where I could remain inconspicuous in case my emotions overcame me, but, to my surprise, Volya caught my eye and motioned me forward to where the elders and warriors were arrayed at the front.

With another shock, I realized that I was a person of importance now. The Horse Master of Draebard. The thought circled my mind like a carrion vulture, refusing to settle. Almost against my own will, I slotted myself next to Andoc—a familiar face amongst a sea of intimidating elders. He wrapped an arm around my shoulders and squeezed for a moment before letting go; it was all I could do not to abandon my tight control and sag against him.

As twilight deepened, the eerie sound of drums broke the near-silence. From the direction of the temple, torches flared into life two at a time along the edge of the main road through the village, coming ever closer. As they approached the green, I could see the surviving acolytes, Reston and Crenelo, lighting the torches in tandem before moving on to the next pair, and the next, and the next. Behind them, Senovo followed with measured steps. Where he had been slumped and weary earlier at the temple barracks as he watched over the High Priest, he now stood straight-backed, his chin high. His eyes were lined with the kohl that had first drawn my attention and admiration when I moved to the village three years ago.

He was, in a word, beautiful.

When the last of the torches arrayed in front of the pyre were lit, sending curls of greasy smoke into the night air, Senovo raised the ceremonial bowl he was carrying high over his head.

"Mighty Deresta, She-Who-Burns," he began, his sonorous voice carrying easily across the green. "Goddess of sunlight. Goddess of immolation. Tonight your children stand before you in grief. We commend our many dead to your purifying caress, that their ashes might return to feed the earth, and their souls might return to the sky, carried upon your smoke."

"*Ever shall it be so,*" chanted the crowd, as one.

Senovo lowered the bowl, balancing it in one hand. He moved to the end of the long pyre and dipped the fingers of the other hand into the sacred oil within, flicking a few drops on the first shrouded figure.

"Wyarra," he said. "Wife of Denuto. Beloved mother and sister." He moved slowly to the next body, flicking more oil. "Cuscan. Mighty warrior. Protector of Draebard even unto death." The next shroud was heartbreakingly small. "Monis. Treasured son and source of great joy… "

Taking his time, Senovo continued around the pyre at a stately pace, his voice never faltering as he recited the names and associations of the dead. Sounds of grief and weeping swelled at some of the names, as bereaved friends and family members were embraced and comforted by those around them. Many of the names belonged to Senovo's fellow priests. Eventually, he reached the final two figures.

"Gretya. Mother and provider not only to her beloved daughters, but to all the village."

Grief swelled in my chest as I remembered a gap-toothed smile and the smell of good food, distributed with love and care. Senovo moved to the final shroud, flicking oil over it.

"Jorun," Senovo said. "Horse Master of Draebard. Caretaker of the herd. Mentor and father to his apprentices."

A choked sound forced its way up from my chest, and I felt suddenly dizzy. Before I could properly begin to panic about making a scene, a strong hand settled on the small of my back. Rested there, quietly. I glanced up through burning eyes at Andoc standing next to me, but he was facing straight ahead, his face a mask.

Senovo turned back to the crowd. "Deresta, accept your faithful children into your embrace. Return them to the earth and sky from whence they came."

"Ever shall it be so," I whispered with the rest of those present, my voice breaking.

The two acolytes circled the pyre, lighting the wood at intervals with a *whoosh* of climbing flames. Within moments, the whole thing was ablaze. It would burn all night.

"Go in peace," Senovo said. "Celebrate the lives that return to the gods this evening. Blessings be upon you all."

He swept into a low bow, rising a moment later. I was not the only one to notice the slight sway of weariness—covered quickly—as Senovo straightened. Beside me, I felt Andoc tense.

"He didn't rest at all, did he?" I asked quietly. "You should go to him."

"I will, once he gets back to the temple barracks." Andoc's hand was still resting on my back. "Will you come?"

I chewed the inside of my lip, surprised by the question, and the offer inherent in it. But... no. The horses needed watching, and I would not distract the two of them from their grief with my own.

"No, I need to return to guard the horses," I said. "I'll meet you at the pens at first light for our journey."

"Very well," he replied, his hand falling away. I tried not to miss it. "We'll see you in the morning, then." He paused. "I'll talk to Volya about setting a night guard on the pens. Should have thought of that earlier, actually."

"We've all been distracted," I said. "It's a good idea, though."

The gathering was already breaking up as people retreated to grieve in private. I lost myself in the dispersing crowd, heading back to my hut to prepare a bedroll and other supplies for the morning. A bit of stale bread and cheese still sat on my table from the supper Andoc had brought me the previous evening, and I forced myself to eat it even though my stomach felt queasy with fatigue and grief. I thought of the people gathered in groups throughout the village, toasting the dead with flagons of wine and ale. Reminiscing. Supporting each other.

Suddenly I felt very cold and alone.

You don't have to be, said a little voice in my head. It was true. I could probably go to the temple barracks right now, to join Senovo and Andoc. What was it High Priest Rhystel had told me about the gods putting doors in front of us?

I stood there for several moments staring at the wall, thinking. Eventually, I shouldered my traveling pack with a sigh and headed for the horse pens.

⁂

My tears that night burned themselves out more quickly than on the previous night, and I slept in fits and starts, waking at every tiny noise. When the first hint of dawn appeared in the east, I felt more fatigued than when I'd curled up in the hay hours ago; my eyes were red and itchy. Another dunk in the horse trough revived me somewhat, but I cringed at the thought of two full days in the saddle. It was no comfort whatsoever that Senovo was probably even worse off than I was.

The lads were staring to arrive as I straightened my rumpled clothing, cursing myself for having forgotten to remove my breast bindings last night. The leather itched horribly, but there was nothing to be done about it now. On a positive note, I was pleased to see Dalon arriving with the very first group—it seemed he was taking his role as the temporary leader seriously. We exchanged wary nods, and I left him to it.

Making my way to the large pen, I grabbed a couple of halters, catching Andoc's long-suffering gelding and a steady, reliable gray mare for Senovo to ride. Kekenu followed along behind us, chewing on a mouthful of hay as he walked. It was soothing to go through the familiar routine of grooming and saddling the horses. With a small flash of vindictive pleasure, I fastened a rope hackamore around Andoc's horse's head, rather than a bitted bridle.

After all, I was the Horse Master now.

The sun was just breaking over the horizon when Andoc and Senovo appeared. They came over and stowed their bedrolls and saddlebags, tying them into place snugly behind the horses' saddles. Andoc reached into one of his bags and handed me a parchment-wrapped pastry drizzled with honey and chopped nuts.

"Because apparently you don't eat unless I feed you," he said. As I eagerly bit into the treat, his eyes were caught by the rope hackamore on his horse's head, and he turned back to me with a raised eyebrow. "Really?"

I gave him a sharp smile in reply.

"She did warn you, you know," Senovo said, looking about as pale and exhausted as I had thought he would.

Within fifteen minutes, the three of us were riding out of town on the eastern road, heading toward the territory of our mysterious, much-reviled neighbors.

"So," I said when the silence threatened to become oppressive, "what exactly makes me so uniquely suited to negotiating with the Mereni?"

Andoc smiled across at me. "I told you. They respect horse tamers."

"*Andoc*," Senovo said, shooting his companion a quelling look.

"What? They do." Andoc's smile gained a faintly secretive edge. "And as for the rest of it, can you blame me for wanting Carivel to see it firsthand?"

Senovo shook his head in disgust and caught my eye. "The Mereni have some fundamentally different views about things that tend not to sit well with most other Eburosi."

"Good thing Carivel's not most Eburosi," Andoc said.

"I am right here, you know," I grumbled. "Fine. Keep your secrets, both of you."

Conversation as we rode was sporadic. Both Senovo and I were still laboring under a cloud of grief, not to mention lack of sleep. I was starting to wonder if Andoc ever showed weakness, or if he always maintained such a disgustingly high level of competence and equanimity. Though, to be fair, he hadn't lost anyone as close to him as Senovo and I had. At least, I didn't think he had.

Predictably, Andoc called a halt and forced us to eat lunch as the sun reached its zenith in the sky.

The chill of the past couple of days had given way to sunny warmth, and we hobbled the horses to let them graze while we sat propped up against tree trunks at the edge of a little clearing, drinking watered wine and eating dried fruit and jerky.

"You two could nap for a while if you like," Andoc said, a few minutes after we'd finished the food and drink.

I forced my eyes open, not having realized they'd closed. Across from me, Senovo rolled his head back and forth against his tree trunk, a lazy negative.

"No," he said. "It's fine."

"We should keep moving," I agreed. "We'll sleep tonight when it's too dark to travel."

Andoc shrugged, as if it was of no matter to him either way. We repacked the horses and continued on. Kekenu was a reassuring, steady presence underneath me. I gained occasional flashes of amusement as Andoc wrestled with his simple rope reins, muttering under his breath. Senovo was a pale and silent figure at my side.

The landscape changed gradually into something unfamiliar. I had never been this far east of Draebard, my own wanderings having taken place to the north of the village I now called home. The east was craggier, with exposed rocks jutting through the ochre-colored soil. Streams were plentiful and fast moving, and we crossed one river that was wider than Draebard's village green and came up to the horses' bellies at the deepest point.

Senovo was looking positively haggard and I was starting to doze off in my saddle when the sun finally slipped below the horizon.

"We should make camp," I said after jerking awake for the dozenth time in the last hour or so.

"And here I was, waiting for you to slip right off of your horse's back before you decided it was time to stop," Andoc said.

I glared at him, raising an eyebrow in my best haughty manner. "Nonsense. A Horse Master is perfectly capable of riding and sleeping at the same time." I blinked as I realized what I'd just said. "Gods. That's going to take a whole lot of getting used to."

"I know the feeling," Senovo said softly — the first words he'd uttered in hours.

We found a likely looking spot at the base of a large boulder set beside a small stream and puttered around, gathering scrub wood and caring for the horses. Senovo sprinkled some powder from a pouch on the kindling and struck a spark, which immediately set the pile to flaming brightly.

"Trade secret," he murmured in response to my impressed noise, feeding larger wood to the flames until the campfire was burning merrily in the deepening dark.

With our bedrolls arranged around the fire and our responsibilities for the day complete, we passed around food and drink, leaning against the seats of our saddles on the ground. The three of us filled our cups with a deep red vintage from a wineskin that Andoc provided. I couldn't suppress a cough as it burned down my throat, shockingly strong.

"Yup—I brought along the good stuff," he said, his smile flashing teeth. "You can thank me later."

"Pass it back," I said when I'd regained control of my voice, motioning for the skin and topping up my clay traveling cup when Senovo handed it to me.

Two cups later, I was feeling positively mellow, and maybe even a bit fuzzy around the edges. So were my companions, if their relaxed slouches were anything to go by. I frowned as my pleasant lassitude was interrupted by discomfort when I changed position. Scratching self-consciously at my midriff—trying to ease the itchiness of my bindings—I had a sudden thought.

"Hang on," I said. "I just realized that you both know my deep, dark secret already. Stay here for a minute. I'm going to go take off the wrap that I use to bind my chest."

Andoc smiled his cocky, albeit slightly drunk smile from across the fire. "Ah... don't be shy, Carivel—I've seen it all before, and Senovo here is a religious man. Not to mention a eunuch."

I ignored the little thrill that ran up my spine at his words in favor of offering him a rude hand gesture I'd learned from Dalon and his friends. When Senovo snorted softly in amusement, I counted it a victory. The firelight didn't quite extend to the creek bed, so I walked to the edge of the water to remove my tunic. The bindings had been on for far too long. Taking them off felt wonderful, even though my skin tingled and ached when the blood flow returned.

The humid evening was still warm enough that I dipped my tunic in the running water and used it to scrub at my face, arms, and torso before rinsing it out and donning it again. The damp material was clammy against my skin, raising gooseflesh and hardening my nipples to painful points before my body heat warmed it. Gathering up the discarded soft leather strips into a loose roll, I returned to the fire. I stuffed the bindings in my saddlebag with a faint flush of embarrassment, and gratefully accepted more of the strong wine.

"It's frankly rather amazing to me that you've been hiding something like this successfully for three years," Andoc said once I'd settled down again and taken a deep draught. "I mean—how did you piss?"

Senovo choked on his wine. I leaned back, giving the question all the careful consideration of the fairly drunk.

"Privately," I replied after a weighty pause.

Andoc laughed aloud, and I let myself appreciate the fine lines crinkling around the corners of his mouth and eyes in the firelight. "Yes," he said, "I imagine that would be the most prudent approach."

Senovo cleared his throat. "This is, of course, from my own personal curiosity, and not something you need to answer if you don't care to, Carivel. But, if you could wake tomorrow with the body of a young man... would you?"

I'd be lying if I said I hadn't thought about it. Some days, it seemed to be all I could think about, if I were being truthful. And yet...

"Maybe?" I said. "I think so. Most of the time, anyway. Even as a small child, I didn't really feel like a girl all that often."

"But you are attracted to men, yes?" Senovo probed gently.

"And eunuchs," Andoc added. I was surprised to see that his teasing smile had faded, leaving him serious.

I couldn't control the flush that stained my cheeks, but despite my drunkenness I was acutely aware that I was in the presence of the only two people in the world with whom I could discuss my life openly.

"Yes," I said. The wine gave me the courage to meet Senovo's eyes and add, "but only the beautiful ones with kind souls and eloquent eyes."

"Ah," Andoc said with a fond look at the young priest next to him, "she has the measure of you, my friend." He frowned, and looked back to me. "Oh... there's a thought. Would you rather we still referred to you as 'he,' Carivel? In private, I mean."

When I opened my mouth to reply, a choked noise that sounded suspiciously close to a sob came out instead. My right hand flew to my mouth to keep anything else from escaping. *The wine*, I thought. *It's the wine, and the grief.* I forced myself to breathe deeply and slowly, not looking at the others as they straightened slightly in concern. I was more thankful than I could say that neither of them tried to approach me in that moment. I think I would have shattered and blown away like a dried puff-flower in the wind at the first kind touch.

"Sorry. I'm sorry," I said when my voice was finally back under my control. "No one has ever given me that choice before."

In twenty-three-and-a-half years, not a single person ever let me choose.

The two men across from me relaxed slightly, letting me feel out the words as I spoke them.

"In a perfect world," I started slowly, "I would have been born a boy. I would have grown up desiring girls; married and had children." Andoc and Senovo shared a look I couldn't decipher. I wasn't sure it was about me at all. "This isn't a perfect world, though. I don't know *what* I am. I desire men. My body is a woman's. My mind is mostly a man's, I think. But I still liked it when you called me 'she.' I think 'she' feels like a kind of freedom to me, after hiding the truth for so long. It will never happen of course, but ideally, I would like it if I didn't have to hide my female body from anyone. If they all knew that I was born a 'she,' but they didn't care that I dressed like a man and cared for the horses and lusted after other men."

It was the most I had ever said out loud about my unfortunate position in my entire life. I worried at my lower lip with my teeth and looked up to meet my companions' eyes.

"That seems an understandable wish," Senovo said easily.

"Very well," said Andoc. "In private, you shall be our good friend, Horse Mistress Carivel, who happens to think and act like a man most of the time, but who lusts uncontrollably after other attractive men. And eunuchs, of course. Personally, I'd love to hear more details about that last part."

The cocky smile had returned. I still wanted to punch it off his face, but between the wine and the soul baring, there was some danger that the punch would be the prelude to an attempt to jump on him and kiss him senseless.

"Too bad," I told him instead. "First, tell me more about yourselves. It's only fair. Andoc, how did you come to be a warrior of Draebard? Senovo, how did you become a priest?"

"*First*?" Andoc echoed. "So there's a chance we might get to hear about your uncontrollable lust afterward?" I glared at him drunkenly. "Fine, fine," he continued with a huff. "There's not much to tell, in my case. I come from Venzor, in the northeast. My father died after falling off our roof when I was thirteen. The idiot was trying to fix a leak during a thunderstorm, of all things. My mother is still alive, as far as I know. I try to visit her at least once a year."

"What brought you to Draebard?" I asked.

Andoc shrugged. "I wanted to be a warrior, but everyone in my village still saw me as the pale, sickly lad I'd been as a child. When I was sixteen, I came here for a fresh start and apprenticed myself to Volya. That's pretty much it, really. Senovo's story is far more interesting than mine, to be honest, though I'm not sure how much of it he'll care to share."

I looked to Senovo with renewed interest.

"How much do you know of initiation into the priesthood?" Senovo asked quietly, his eyes on the wine in his cup.

"Just what everyone knows, I suppose," I replied, intrigued. "You have to choose to become a eunuch, giving up your ability to sire children so that you can act as a neutral party during rites of fertility and so forth. It always seemed like a huge sacrifice to make, to me at least. Though I suppose some priests do end up becoming very powerful people."

"A slightly simplistic view, but essentially correct," Senovo allowed.

I looked at him shrewdly. "You don't want power, though. You said as much."

"Definitely not," Senovo replied.

"So why choose to become a eunuch? I've always thought that must be a horrible thing to go through."

"I didn't," he said.

"You... didn't?" Perhaps it was the wine addling my wits, but that didn't make any sense. I told him as much.

Senovo's eyes grew distant. "I was born south of here. Far to the south, in fact. Things are different there." Andoc, who had become very quiet, eased closer until his shoulder was brushing the priest's as he continued. "My family was extremely poor. My grandfather had gone deeply into debt with the moneylenders. My mother and father were still trying to escape from under it, while also feeding me and my five older brothers and sisters. I'm afraid I was a rather difficult boy.

Wild. Always escaping my chores and disappearing into the woods on my own—"

"It was the wolf in you," Andoc said.

"Perhaps. Whatever the case, the year of my seventh birthday, the harvest was even worse than usual. In their desperation, my parents decided to sell me to the priest's guild."

I drew in a sharp breath. "Your parents *sold* you? A child? How was that even allowed?"

Senovo lifted one shoulder and let it fall, staring into the fire. "It's just the way things are in the south. In certain circumstances, people can become commodities. I was in service to the guild for ten years, and hated every minute of it. When I reached the age of seventeen, I received the *honor* of initiation. Even though it meant I would no longer be a slave, it was not an honor I desired *in the least*, to put it mildly. Unfortunately, my opinion in the matter was not consulted."

"That's terrible," I said, barely able to wrap my mind around such a thing. "I think that may be the most terrible thing I've ever heard."

"Four of them held me down," Senovo continued, and his eyes were very far away now. Andoc's arm came up across the priest's shoulders, gripping him lightly as Senovo continued in a flat voice. "They forced a thick leather strap into my mouth so I wouldn't bite through my own tongue. When I was completely restrained, the high priest crushed my scrotum between two lengths of oak board with a heavy mallet."

"He deserved to die for that," Andoc said, and I got the impression it wasn't the first time he'd spoken the words.

Senovo continued as if he had not heard. "The shock and pain caused me to shift into the form of the wolf for the first time in my life. I savaged the priests holding me down, ripped open the high priest's stomach, and escaped from the temple into the wildlands beyond. When I changed back, days later, I was alone and naked, in excruciating agony. I crawled to the nearest road and told the first farmer who passed that I'd been attacked and robbed by bandits. When I'd recovered enough to travel, I started walking north and didn't stop until I reached a land where they didn't buy and sell children. Somewhere no one knew me—where I could start over. Of course, my options for making a livelihood at that point were fairly, shall we say, *narrow*. You see the result before you now."

The silence stretched for several moments.

"I'm deeply sorry," I said eventually. "Perhaps I shouldn't have asked in the first place, but I'm honored that you would share something so personal with me, nonetheless. You have my word that your story will travel no further."

"A secret for a secret," Senovo said, echoing his words from yesterday. He turned to Andoc, his level voice never wavering. "Tonight will be bad, my friend. Don't let me change."

Andoc nodded and pressed a kiss to Senovo's forehead. Senovo closed his eyes and leaned into the contact for a moment before pulling back, wrapping himself in his bedroll, and turning his back to the fire. A few minutes later he was fast asleep.

"Don't be afraid of anything you see or hear tonight," Andoc said. "Senovo is far more frightened of the wolf than you or I have cause to be."

"The wolf saved my life," I said. "I don't fear it."

Andoc nodded. His faint smile was sad. "Of course you don't. Good night, Horse Mistress Carivel. Things will look better in the light of morning."

"Good night, Andoc," I replied. "Take care of him tonight."

"I always do."

SEVEN

The night was pleasant, and the wine combined with my exhaustion should have rendered me utterly insensible until morning. Instead, I jerked awake in the small hours, the dregs of a half-forgotten dream lying bitter on the back of my tongue. The fire had burned down to glowing coals, casting a faint orange light over the figures across from me. A low sound — almost a snarl — prickled the hair at the back of my neck, and I sat up slowly.

"Not tonight, my friend," Andoc said. "I do not give you leave to change."

The warrior was bare-chested, propped up on one arm so he could look down at Senovo's huddled form next to him.

"*I can't stop it,*" Senovo said, and he did, indeed, sound terrified at the prospect of freeing the animal caged within himself.

"I'm not giving you a choice in the matter, *amadi*," Andoc said, and my chest constricted at the endearment. "You will not hunt tonight."

The rumbling growl came again. I caught my breath in shock as Senovo surged up, his hands reaching for Andoc's face and throat like claws. The warrior batted them away, seemingly without effort. There was a quick twist of bodies that I couldn't quite follow in the low light, and then he was straddling Senovo's hips, one hand pinning the priest's wrists over his head, and the other pressing against his vulnerable neck.

"Yield, my friend," Andoc said, not even out of breath as Senovo strained against him. "I told you before, you get no choice in this tonight."

After a tense moment that had me holding my breath, Senovo… *melted*; there was no other word for it. All the tension flowed from his muscles. His head tilted back, baring his throat to Andoc's callused hand like an offering.

"There you are, dear one. That's better, isn't it?" Andoc said, a soft smile crossing his face. The hands pinning Senovo loosened their grip, becoming a caress, and the priest arched into the contact with a soft noise of surrender. My eyes were drawn of their own volition to the outline of Andoc's stiff prick, tenting the soft leather of his breeches as Senovo's torso twisted beneath him restlessly. A flood of wetness pulsed between my own legs at the sight. When I dragged my eyes back up to Andoc's face, he was looking at me with one side of his mouth quirked up in half a smile.

"Carivel is awake, *amadi*," he said, leaning close to Senovo's ear. "She's watching you yield to me. I think she likes what she sees."

Senovo and I shivered in reaction to the words at the same time, and the sound that the eunuch made was almost a whine.

"Shh," Andoc said. "There's plenty of time for all that later." His eyes flicked to mine briefly as he spoke. "Tonight, we sleep."

The flesh between my thighs was throbbing as I watched Senovo nuzzle into Andoc's side, the warrior easing himself back down into his sleeping roll with an arm draped possessively around his friend. If I'd been a man in body as well as mind, my cock would have been hard enough to pound stone at the sight. I silently lowered myself back down into my own nest of blankets, unable to keep from rocking the heel of my hand against the crotch of my breeches to try to ease the pressure.

It was a testament to my own exhaustion that I fell asleep again a few minutes later, the scene between the two of them playing over in my mind, following me down into dreams.

⚜

The following morning should have been awkward. Instead, Senovo awoke with a groan, stretching—looking more rested than I'd seen him since the attack. Seeming to remember the events of the night, he froze, looking at me.

"All right?" he asked, watching me with what might have been nervousness.

I nodded. "You?" I asked.

He nodded in return.

"Of course we're all right," Andoc said in a voice far too cheerful for the early hour. "It's a beautiful morning, everyone finally got some decent sleep, and I'm possibly one step closer to hearing more details about Carivel's uncontrollable lust. What could be better?"

"I never said it was uncontrollable," I grumbled, glaring at him even as I blushed scarlet. "Senovo, is he always like this?"

"Always," Senovo replied.

By unspoken consent, we kept to neutral topics as we readied ourselves for the second day of travel. Something about daylight (or perhaps sobriety) did not lend itself as well to discussing private matters as a campfire after dark did. Instead, I attempted to pry more information from Andoc regarding the Mereni, and was once again deflected.

It was cooler than the previous day, with clouds blocking the sun most of the time. As the afternoon wore on, we were pelted with occasional fat raindrops. We'd been riding in the higher elevations for more than a day, but now we were once again descending. The fertile valleys below, while not identical to those around Draebard, were at least more familiar looking than the scrubby uplands had been.

Beneath me, Kekenu suddenly perked up with interest, lifting his head to gaze to our left with pricked ears. In the distance, I made out a herd of horses. Even from here I could see that they were taller and more slender-legged than the animals I was used to.

"The horses look different here," I said, standing in the stirrups to get a better view.

Andoc nodded. "Mereni horses have a reputation for being as fast as the wind... not to mention rank as hell."

"Perhaps that's why they respect horse tamers so much," Senovo said.

"Maybe so," Andoc agreed, turning his attention back to me. "Carivel, I know I've been playing things close to my chest, but you should know there's a chance the Leader will ask you to prove your skills on a difficult horse."

"That's fine," I said, unconcerned. A thought occurred to me. "Is he likely to ask either of you two to prove *your* skills as well?"

"It's very possible," Senovo replied.

"Hmm... this may end up being quite an interesting trip," I said.

⚜

The village of the Mereni was considerably larger than Draebard. We arrived an hour or so before dusk and entered by the main road, riding side by side. While we received a number of curious looks with our strange clothing and short, thickset riding horses, no one challenged us until Andoc dismounted outside what I assumed was the village meeting hall. He handed his horse off to me and approached the door, only to find his way barred by an extraordinarily tall man and an extraordinarily tall woman flanking the entrance.

"State your business," said the woman.

I was surprised to see that she wore loose leather trousers with a bronze short sword at her waist, and that the man with her seemed content to let her lead the discussion. The woman's long hair was an unusual shade of fiery red; her features were sharp and strong. Andoc appeared unfazed by her presence, but I couldn't help but find amusement in the fact that he had to look up slightly to meet her eyes.

"Greetings," Andoc said. "My friends and I have traveled two days from the west to meet with the esteemed Leader of the Mereni. I apologize that we were unable to send word ahead. Could you perhaps arrange for a message to be delivered?"

To my surprise, he sounded positively mature and diplomatic. I found myself strangely impressed by it.

"What's the message?" asked the woman.

"My companions and I have come at the behest of Chief Volya of Draebard to discuss an alliance against the Alyrion Empire. Alyrion troops attacked our village in the dead of night four days ago, killing and wounding dozens."

"Draebard, eh?" the woman said, looking us up and down with an expression of distaste. "I'll let Magoldis know. Can't promise much beyond that."

"That's all I ask," Andoc said, the picture of charm. "In the mean time, is there somewhere that the three of us might stay for the night? A tavern or a way-house?"

"Try Harinel's place. He lets rooms. Keep heading east, and turn right at the second road. It's the house with the yellow door. I'll send a messenger there in the morning if Magoldis agrees to see you."

Andoc bowed and offered his thanks. As I returned his horse to him, I said, "You should try employing some of that charm with your friends, you know, instead of saving it all for complete strangers."

The warrior scoffed, a twinkle in his eye. "Nonsense," he said. "It's far too much effort. With my friends, I prefer to rely on my rugged good looks for most things."

Harinel, when we found him, turned out to be a stooped old man with one eye missing. His house was ramshackle and crook-cornered, but the inside was spacious and relatively clean.

"I only have one room available tonight," he said. "Will that suit you?"

Senovo and Andoc both looked to me, and I shrugged my agreement. It wasn't appreciably different from sharing a campfire with them, and at this point I didn't have any secrets left for them to discover, to be perfectly honest.

After paying Harinel for the room, we unsaddled the horses and let them loose in the small pen behind the house, where they had access to hay and a shallow wooden trough full of water. Senovo and I were still suffering the ill effects of several nights of grief and poor sleep, so Andoc offered to venture out alone to procure food and drink for us.

When we were alone, I broached the topic that had been hanging between us all day.

"Senovo," I began, "I want to apologize for invading your privacy with Andoc last night. I hope it didn't make you terribly uncomfortable knowing that I was watching. I realize I should have left, or at least turned away. I'm sorry. I just—

I wasn't expecting it, I guess, and I didn't really understand what I was seeing."

Senovo sat down on the edge of one of the low beds, giving me his full attention. I forced myself to meet his piercing green eyes and hold them.

"I didn't mind," he said. "In fact, I'm afraid to say that when I get like that, a bit of additional humiliation rather enhances the experience. Did it bother you?"

"It… probably should have?" I said, losing my battle to maintain eye contact. My hands twisted together in my lap; I looked down at them instead. "Andoc was right, though. I liked it. It was beautiful. Exciting. Even if I don't really understand why."

I darted an uncertain glance at Senovo, who appeared unperturbed. I was forcibly reminded that he was a priest, and a good one—however horrific his introduction to that life might have been. Dealing with matters related to relationships and sex was a huge part of what priests did, whether in a ceremonial context or counseling couples regarding their mutual pleasure and harmony. If the fact that the current discussion was personal bothered him, he certainly didn't show it.

"Would I be correct in assuming that your unusual circumstances mean you have not had much experience with physical love in its various forms?" he asked tactfully.

I snorted softly. "Not unless you count my own fingers in the dark." I paused for a moment, remembering. "Well. I also kissed a girl once, back in my old village. I was very young at the time. I had to see if I could want girls, like a proper boy. It didn't work."

"A reasonable experiment," Senovo replied. "In addition to the pleasure of purely physical touch, you may or may not have discovered that sexuality relies rather heavily on the mind. In the case of eunuchs, I think I can safely say that when sexuality persists at all, it becomes largely a mental exercise."

I thought of the fantasies that often played out behind my eyelids while I touched myself, and blushed faintly. It didn't help that most of those fantasies involved the very person sitting across from me.

Senovo smiled—a brief uptick of one side of his mouth. "I see the concept is not completely foreign to you."

I cleared my throat. "Not completely, no."

"Suffice to say, if you can imagine something—and even if you can't—there is probably someone who finds it arousing. What you saw last night was the way in which Andoc and I fit together. I do not feel desire in the way that undamaged men and women do; that was taken from me the day that my genitals were crushed by the men who owned me. While I can still feel physical pleasure from some forms of sexual contact, and while I happily engage in those sorts of practices with Andoc, the true gift that he gives me is control of the wolf."

"How?" I asked. "Last night, you asked him not to let you change, but surely that's something only you can control?"

"The wolf is stronger than me," Senovo said, "but Andoc is stronger than the wolf."

"I still don't understand," I said, frowning.

"Wolves in packs live within a strictly enforced hierarchy. The strongest control the pack, and the weaker wolves submit to them willingly—though a struggle for dominance may ensue at any time if a submissive wolf senses weakness in one of its superiors." Senovo paused, as if searching for the best way to put something into words. "When the wolf submits to Andoc, and Andoc forbids me to change, I don't change. It's not even a struggle. I can relax, safe in the knowledge that I will remain human. It is, perhaps, the *only* time I can truly relax, and as such, I treasure it. And him."

Something clicked within my thoughts. "The night of the attack..." I began, and he nodded.

"Andoc had been gone for days," he said, "and I was weak. I shifted."

"You saved my life," I pointed out.

"Awakening the next morning with a man's flesh in my belly, and his lifeblood smeared across my face," he added.

It was actually rather horrific when he described it that way. Not knowing what else to say, I said, "I'm sorry."

"I'm not sorry I saved you, Carivel," he said. "Never think that."

I nodded, not knowing what to do with the emotions welling up in my chest. Ever the coward, I changed the subject. "So being with Andoc lets you relax and stop fighting the wolf for awhile. I can understand the power of that, I think. And he... what? Likes controlling people? Being in charge?" I remembered the sight of Andoc straddling Senovo's hips, his erection jutting visibly within his breeches as he pinned the priest in place. Desire twisted shamefully in my belly, even now.

"He's a young, strong man, and a warrior," Senovo said. "I suppose he enjoys the struggle — the physical victory — but honestly, his pleasure seems to come mainly from meeting my needs. My need for him... for his strength and care."

"Pfft," came Andoc's familiar voice from the doorway, "Nonsense. I just like rolling around on the ground while rubbing up against a sweaty, writhing body. I mean, what's not to like?"

Mortification flooded me as he entered, swinging the door shut behind him with one foot. Still, I should have guessed that the infuriating prat would actually relish the idea of his sex life being discussed in his absence. His grin was wide as he deposited an armload of food wrapped in large, waxy green leaves on the room's rickety table. A moment later, the mouth-watering smell of roasted meat filled the room.

"So," he said as he removed the strap of a wineskin from over his shoulder and uncorked it, "we're finally discussing Carivel's uncontrollable lust, then? You two could have waited for me, you know."

He took a deep drink from the skin and passed it to Senovo, looking back and forth between us for all the world as if he were watching an archery contest or a wrestling match playing out on the village green for his entertainment. My deep-seated desire to punch him on the nose reared its ugly head once again.

Instead, somewhat surprised at my own courage, I said, "Yes, in fact I was just about to jump on Senovo and stick my tongue down his throat when you so rudely interrupted."

Senovo released a faint sound of amusement, and Andoc laughed deep and long. "Well, I'd be a hypocrite if I tried to blame you for that," said the warrior. "He is rather irresistible, isn't he?"

"Only to those with no self-control, I think you'll find," Senovo said in a wry voice. His own thirst sated, he passed the wineskin across to me.

Sensing that a certain degree of drunkenness would probably help with this conversation, I tipped it up and let the warm drink flow down my throat, enjoying its mellow taste. While Andoc might infuriate me on a regular basis, I had to admit that the man knew his wines. Corking the skin and putting it aside, I tore into one of the chunks of meat threaded onto a peeled wooden skewer. It was delicious… tender pork covered in some kind of unfamiliar spice.

"Now that we've finally gotten the 'lust' conversation out of the way," Andoc said around a mouthful of food, "you do realize it's only a matter of time until I convince you to act on it."

I… *wait, what*? I blinked, frozen in place with the meat held in front of my lips.

"You have all the subtlety of a bull in heat, Andoc," said Senovo.

"Bulls don't go into heat, *amadi*. Cows do," Andoc replied, unrepentant. "I thought you were supposed to know about these things, being a priest and all."

"Wait, *what*?" I said, my mouth finally catching up with my brain.

"I said, it's only a matter of time until I convince you to act on your uncontrollable lust," Andoc repeated slowly, as if I were hard of hearing.

"But…" I said, evidently trying to dazzle them both with my brilliance, "but, you and Senovo already have each other."

Senovo looked up from his skewer of pork. "While it's generally accepted for a young man to dally with a eunuch, the expectation is that he will eventually move on to find a woman and settle down."

I stared at him, appalled. While I knew as well as anyone that many young men and women gained their initial sexual experience from casual liaisons with acolytes and younger members of the priesthood, there was something almost… *blasphemous* about the idea of Andoc one day casting Senovo aside like some youthful folly.

Andoc rolled his eyes at both of us, and said, "However, in this case, since I have absolutely no intention of *moving on* from him, as Senovo so blithely puts it, I suppose I'll just have to find someone who lusts after both of us. Preferably uncontrollably."

I was still staring at him, relief on Senovo's behalf and irritation on my own behalf swirling together like water and wine in a cup. I think my mouth was open.

Senovo sighed. "I'd offer to hit him for you since I'm closer, but as a priest, that sort of thing is frowned upon. Also, we've already established that he's stronger than me."

"No need," I said faintly. "I think I'd rather do it myself."

Andoc lounged back, completely unconcerned. "Except you're worried you'd end up kissing me immediately afterward, am I right?"

Gods. Maybe strangling him would be more satisfying than hitting him.

"Keep telling yourself that," I managed.

"Oh, I intend to picture it quite vividly as I'm falling asleep later. As I suspect you will be," Andoc said, still smiling.

"*Enough*, Andoc," Senovo said. "Carivel, I should warn you that I'm going to need Andoc's help again tonight. If it bothers you, we can try to find someplace else to stay, and leave you in peace."

This was something of a moment of truth, and I was well aware of it. Andoc was looking at me with interest, though he hadn't refuted Senovo's words or offered any more infuriating comments of his own. It reinforced what I already believed — he might tease and push and prod, but Andoc had no intention of taking what was not freely offered. Helpless desire for both of them rose within me, utterly beyond my control.

Deresta's *tits*. I was so far gone for these two that it wasn't even funny.

"I already told you it didn't bother me," I said to Senovo, giving into the inevitable. "I thought it was beautiful, and that was even before I understood it. Besides, you said knowing I was watching helped."

Andoc was looking between the two of us with a speculative gaze, obviously curious about the conversation he'd missed. To his credit and my surprise, though, he didn't say a word.

Senovo nodded. "If it gives you pleasure, then I'm pleased. The gods smile on us when we utilize their gifts in such a way. As long as you know that you can leave at any time if you don't like something."

"You won't leave, though," Andoc said confidently.

Bastard. He was probably right. I ignored him, and assured Senovo that I understood. The three of us finished our meal in silence, Senovo growing visibly more distant as we did. I was beginning to understand that his distraction was the outward sign of his internal struggle for control. Andoc cleared away the remains of the meal and went to check the horses. While he was gone, I turned my back to Senovo and stripped off my tunic, unwrapping my breasts with a quiet sigh of relief. Pulling the tunic back on, I took off my boots and breeches and made myself comfortable on the smaller of the two beds, wearing only my shirt and smallclothes.

"Are you all right?" I asked Senovo, who still seemed to be off in a world of his own.

"Yes, I'm fine," he said faintly, eyes closed. "Merely very tired."

"You're stronger than you think," I told him, not entirely sure where the words were coming from. "Andoc will be back soon, though, and you can rest for awhile."

I watched in fascination as a faint tremor traveled through the priest's body, his face creasing for an instant with pain and longing.

"Yes," he agreed.

Andoc arrived a few moments later, a couple of coils of rope from the saddlebags looped over his shoulder. His smile at me was subdued, and he crossed immediately to Senovo's side, dropping the rope on the bed next to him.

"It's almost dark, *amadi*," he said, "and the candle is barely a stub. Give me a few moments to light a fire so I can watch over you properly."

"I could do that," I offered belatedly, berating myself for not having thought of it earlier.

Andoc shook his head. "No, you're already comfortable, and I don't mind. It won't take long."

I nodded, remembering what Senovo had said about Andoc wanting to care for others. Though he lacked Senovo's magic fire-starting powder, it wasn't long before he was feeding wood to a small pile of burning kindling, and soon a merry little blaze was crackling away in the hearth, lighting the room with a warm, flickering glow.

Andoc rose from the fire and returned to the bed, grazing Senovo's cheek with the backs of his fingers. "It's time, *amadi*," he said. "Take your clothes off and kneel on the bed."

I caught my breath silently. Already, this was different than the previous night. Senovo rose slowly and undid the fastenings at the front of his traveling robes. The heavy fabric slid from his shoulders, pooling on the rough wooden planks of the floor. Beneath, he wore breeches and boots for riding, but no tunic or linen undershirt. His chest was smooth and flat. Hairless.

Without hesitation, he unfastened the laces of his trousers. Sitting on the edge of the bed, he toed off his soft boots, and stood again to slide the breeches down to his ankles and off. His linen smallclothes followed a moment later, leaving him bare to my fascinated gaze as he gracefully folded himself into a kneeling position on the straw-filled mattress as if in prayer.

I had seen plenty of boys' pricks in my years working for Jorun. Most of the lads thought nothing of whipping themselves out to take a piss against the trunk of a convenient tree. And of course, I'd attended fertility ceremonies and handfastings throughout my life—though never, obviously, as a participant. I'd seen young men skinny-dipping, and warriors sparring in breechclouts—including Andoc himself—bare-skinned and sweating.

Senovo's body was the same, but different. His frame was slender, but he carried a sleek layer of fat under his smooth skin, like a river otter. Aside from his dark, perfectly arched eyebrows and the heavy plait of hair hanging from the back of his head, the only hair I could see on his body was a small patch between his legs—much finer and downier than that of the un-castrated males I'd seen.

His prick was small and limp, resting nestled between his thighs as he knelt. Where a man's balls would normally hang, there was only a flap of wrinkled skin, barely visible in the dim light.

Andoc paced slowly around the bed until he was at the priest's back, brushing his fingertips softly over Senovo's shoulders. "I'm going to tie you tonight. How do you want it?"

"Tight," Senovo said, sounding strained. "Please. Make it tight. Don't let it get free."

I caught my breath as Andoc's hand closed over the back of Senovo's neck, guiding him down until he was lying on his stomach, the side of his face pressed into the bed.

"Very well, my friend. Now. Stay there." Andoc's voice was uncompromising as he removed his hand and picked up the first coil of rope. Looping one end around Senovo's left wrist, he pulled both of the priest's arms straight down and back, binding them together behind his body tightly enough that his elbows nearly touched. Andoc quickly retrieved the second length of rope and used it to tie Senovo's knees and ankles together snugly, leaving a single long tail free.

With his grip on the rope's tail, he bent Senovo's knees and pulled his ankles up until they were even with his wrists, fastening his limbs together in a hogtie. There was still some rope left, and Andoc wove it into Senovo's single braid of hair, using the plait as a handhold to force Senovo's head up and back. He adjusted the length between the eunuch's head and ankles carefully, shortening it by increments until Senovo let out a deep groan, his spine bowed in a graceful arch. A shiver skated along my arms as Andoc tied the rope off and stepped back, raising gooseflesh in its wake.

When the warrior pulled a wicked looking dagger from his belt and set it on the table by the bed, I sucked in an audible breath, my eyes flying to his face.

"For the ropes. Just in case," he said patiently. I nodded, feeling ridiculously inexperienced and stupid.

Andoc's full attention returned immediately to the figure on the bed, as did mine. I had a fairly solid understanding of using ropes as restraint; it wasn't unusual for us to tie up a horse's leg to prevent it kicking out while an injury was treated, for instance. I could see immediately the strain Andoc's bonds put on Senovo's body, forcing it into a tense, unnatural position. I suspected it was no coincidence that it also showed off his slender lines in a most appealing manner—I could almost imagine some artist carving the elegant shape laid out before me into wood or bone.

The priest was trembling visibly with the effort of holding himself still, his eyes wide but unseeing. Andoc reached down, fisting the thick plait of hair and using it to force Senovo's head back even further with a slow, inexorable pull. He leaned over, his lips nearly touching the eunuch's ear as he growled, "*Let go.*"

I clamped my legs together around the throbbing pulse at the juncture of my thighs, trembling nearly as hard as Senovo. The priest keened; the noise tailing off to a whine, and then to harsh panting as he writhed and struggled against the rope like a wild animal. Andoc stepped back, staying within easy reach of both the knife and the bound man, his attention never wavering.

Harsh, choked growls echoed around the room, and I quailed as the firelight seemed to momentarily reflect off gray fur rather than golden skin. Andoc was intent but seemingly unconcerned, letting his captive struggle and sob and howl for what seemed like an age, until Senovo's movements eventually grew heavy and slow with exhaustion.

"Enough," Andoc said, steadying Senovo's head with one hand looped casually around his throat. "You're done now, *amadi.*"

Whether Senovo was done or not, I certainly was—shaking as hard as the priest beneath my rough blanket, and feeling as out of breath as if I'd been the one fighting the ropes. My skin felt tight and hot, as if it would combust if someone were to touch me. I was glad Andoc was completely focused on Senovo—I didn't think I could take a teasing comment right now… or even a simple question about my well-being.

Gods. Did Senovo suffer like this *every night*?

The priest was huffing little sobbing breaths, his throat moving against the gentle pressure of Andoc's hand. I watched as he slowly went limp under Andoc's care, his muscles loosening one by one; shallow panting transforming into something slower. Deeper. Andoc eased his hand away, leaving Senovo lying on his belly quietly. The eunuch gradually relaxed into the pressure of the rope, accepting it rather than fighting it.

"That's it," Andoc said softly. "You don't need to fight."

"*Please...*" Senovo whispered hoarsely.

I didn't know what he was asking for, though I doubted anyone with a heart could have denied Senovo whatever he needed at that moment. Fortunately, Andoc seemed to know exactly what was being requested.

"Of course, *amadi*," he said, and began to run one hand over Senovo's body with smooth, gentle strokes. The priest sighed and softened even further into the ropes' embrace, visibly soaking up Andoc's soothing touch. Andoc's hand roamed everywhere, giving equal attention to areas both intimate and platonic—his shoulders, his flanks, the crease of his buttocks.

My desire, which had fled completely in the face of Senovo's desperate, animal struggles, flowed back like a warm tide as I watched callused fingers running over smooth skin. It crested higher when Andoc moved his hand to caress Senovo's face and the priest rooted forward enough to pull the warrior's fingers into his mouth, heedless of the rope pulling his hair tighter against his scalp he suckled in utter contentment.

He would do that to Andoc's prick if he could only reach it, I thought, and couldn't stop the faint moan that escaped my lips.

"Touch yourself if you want to, Carivel," Andoc said, though his attention never wavered from his willing captive. "You're hardly going to offend us at this point."

I... *couldn't*, though. Andoc might tease and prod, intimating that the three of us could be together somehow. But it was all a lie. I was a pariah, and if either of them attached themselves to me, they would be as well. To pretend otherwise was simply cruel.

"What about you?" I asked, to deflect him. "Aren't you going to take your pleasure?"

Andoc shook his head, still not looking away from Senovo as he carefully pulled his fingers free. "He needs me clear-headed when it's this bad. Besides, it would be incredibly crass of me when you're still not completely committed to the idea of being with us, don't you think? You consented to stay while Senovo submitted to me — just like last night. We didn't say anything about sex."

The idea of being with us, he'd said, as if it was a real thing — a thing that could actually happen. Another little splinter of feeling pricked at my heart. *It can never be*, I told myself firmly. Aloud, I asked, "Is it always this bad for him?"

Andoc supported the priest's head with a gentle hand cupped under his chin, taking the strain out of the rope tied to his braided hair. He smoothed his other hand over Senovo's forehead, his thumb massaging slow circles against the priest's temple. "Not always," he said. "When he's tired, when he's upset. He's both right now — we all are. When he's been fighting the change for too long. I think if he ever stopped fighting the wolf and accepted it as part of himself, it wouldn't strain him so."

"Maybe someday he'll see what we do," I said quietly.

Andoc nodded. Beside him, Senovo had gone utterly slack, appearing nearly asleep within the ropes' embrace. The warrior shifted and began to untie him. I could see that he had used slipknots, and they slid free easily enough, even though Senovo had pulled them tight in his struggles. The priest slumbered on, seemingly oblivious, even as Andoc pulled the last of the rope free and eased his limbs into a more comfortable position.

"Will he be all right now?" I asked.

"Yes," said Andoc. "He'll sleep tonight. That should help with things for awhile."

"I'm glad. Goodnight, Andoc."

"Goodnight, Carivel."

My own sleep was slow to come despite my continued exhaustion. When I finally succumbed, disturbing dreams played out behind my eyelids, vivid in their detail. At one point, Jorun and Gretya rose, blood-covered, from their twisted resting places in Jorun's hut and pointed at me accusingly, staring with empty eye sockets.

Your fault, they seemed to say. *You lied to us. You brought this curse down upon us... the gods' punishment for your unnatural inclinations.*

I shuddered awake with a cry of fear on my lips and tears on my face as I sat up and struggled for breath.

The embers of the fire cast a faint glow in the darkness, and a figure shifted in the bed across from me.

"Carivel?" Andoc's voice was groggy—newly awakened. He rose, his silhouette crossing the room. The bed creaked as his weight settled on the edge. He reached toward me as if to place a hand on my shoulder, but I knocked it away in a near panic, still gasping out sobs.

"Don't—" I croaked, unsure what exactly I was warning him against. *Don't make me show more weakness in front of you. Don't make me need you more than I already do.*

Andoc froze, and slowly pulled his hand back. Instead, he eased himself off of the bed to sit beside it, leaning back against the wooden frame. "Very well," he said. "I'll just sit here for awhile, shall I?"

I couldn't answer; it needed all of my focus to stay silent as I cried. True to his word, Andoc said nothing, remaining a solid but unobtrusive presence nearby. Eventually, the tears subsided, leaving me with a throbbing headache. It was not enough to prevent me from sliding back into sleep, though, clogged nose and all.

It was Senovo who woke me many hours later with a light shake of my shoulder. I grunted and rolled up on an elbow, disoriented in the gray morning light. The feeling of red, swollen eyes and phlegm clogging my throat was becoming depressingly familiar after days of grief, but my surroundings were not.

"We're in Meren," Senovo reminded me, correctly interpreting my confused expression.

Meren. Yes. Right. I nodded understanding, and the rest of it came flooding back as I awoke more fully. I cast an assessing gaze over Senovo's form. He looked considerably better than I felt, except for the faint red rope mark barely visible on his wrist, below the sleeve of his robe. I hoped that meant he'd slept soundly through the night.

"Where's Andoc?" I asked, looking around the room.

"Three guesses," Senovo said, a wry note entering his voice.

I let out a little huff of what might have been laughter. "Getting food?"

"Of course. Where else?" Senovo said. He indicated a large wooden bowl sitting on a table next to the room's single window. "There's water if you want to wash."

He made no other mention of my obviously tear-stained face, for which I was very grateful.

"Thanks," I said, rising. The water was cool and helped clear my head. I pulled on my breeches and took my leave to check the horses and relieve myself in a private corner of the pen, away from prying eyes.

When I returned, I was feeling considerably more like a human being except for the low, throbbing headache that had plagued me since my injury during the battle. A young girl was just leaving the room as I re-entered, and I twisted to the side to let her past through the narrow doorway. Inside, Andoc handed me a chunk of coarse, dark bread with dried fruit baked into it.

"Who was that?" I asked.

"Messenger from Magoldis," Andoc said around his own mouthful of food. "We're to present ourselves at the meeting hall in half an hour. Apparently we merit an audience after all."

⚜

The three of us walked back to the meeting hall a few minutes later rather than take the time to groom and saddle the horses. The tall woman from the previous evening was once again guarding the entrance, though the man across from her was a different one.

"Good morning," Andoc greeted her. "Thank you for passing on our message."

The woman eyed him up and down. "Don't mention it," she said, her stony expression never flickering. "Go inside. Magoldis is waiting in the first room."

Andoc sketched a shallow bow and led the way through the door, into the large building. Senovo and I followed, tipping our heads to the guards as we passed. The entryway was at one end of a low-ceilinged hallway, which opened out into a spacious room with a large table surrounded by heavy chairs. Another large, muscular woman sat in one of them, facing the doorway. She was older than the female guard outside, but they shared the same shade of striking red hair and there was a similarity to their features, which made me think that they were probably related. She was also alone in the room.

It was odd seeing women in and around a meeting hall. I wondered if this was the Leader's wife, sent to entertain us until the Leader himself arrived.

"Magoldis," Andoc said next to me, bowing low. "It is our honor to meet with you. Thank you for agreeing to see us on such short notice."

I stared at him for a blank second or two. *This* was Magoldis? Magoldis, leader of the Mereni, was... a woman?

EIGHT

The woman in question rose from her chair and circled the table to stand before us. I felt Senovo's hand touch my elbow, the faint brush of fingers breaking me free of my shocked immobility. Senovo bowed as Magoldis' eyes moved over him, and I quickly followed suit.

"Varanis said you'd come from Draebard, at old Volya's request," Magoldis said, her attention returning to Andoc. Her voice was low and pleasant, but with an underlying steel.

"That is correct," Andoc said. "Our village was attacked in the dead of night a few days ago. The Alyrion commander who took over an abandoned hill-fort west of Draebard drew the Chief and half of the warriors away from the settlement on the pretense of a parlay, only to send soldiers in to attack while the villagers were vulnerable."

"A cowardly act," Magoldis agreed, though her tone gave away nothing. "I notice that Volya did not think meeting with me was important enough for him to come in person."

Senovo stepped forward. "Leader Magoldis, Chief Volya could not allow the village to appear vulnerable again so soon after the last attack. We have many seriously injured, including the High Priest. Most of the temple priests and acolytes are dead. Our Chief meant no disrespect to you,

Leader. However, he had to put the people of Draebard first."

Magoldis raised an eyebrow. "Very pretty words, priest. So, who has Volya sent to speak to me in his stead? A warrior, a priest, and… ?"

The Leader's eyes raked over me, and I froze again, my thoughts still spinning in rapid circles. Andoc rescued me by beginning the introductions.

"I am Andoc, First Among Warriors in Draebard," he said. "This is Senovo, the most senior of the surviving priests excepting the High Priest himself."

"And you said the High Priest was injured?" Magoldis asked.

"Gravely," Senovo answered in a soft voice.

I knew next to nothing of the politics between tribes, beyond the obvious — who was feuding with who, who was allied with who. Nonetheless, I could begin to understand what Volya had done. In his own absence, he had sent his most powerful warrior and likely replacement, the soon-to-be High Priest of the village, and the Horse Master. While two of the three of us might not have come to terms with our new status yet, it was undeniably a dramatic gesture.

Still, the bad blood between Volya and Magoldis — whose society dared to put women in power — was obvious. Looking at Magoldis' stony mien, I wasn't at all sure it would be enough to sway her after years of disagreement and distrust.

The Leader's eyes returned to me. "And this is?" she asked.

The question was directed to Andoc, but before he could answer, I straightened proudly and uttered the nine most reckless words I had ever said in my life.

"Leader Magoldis, I am Carivel, Horse Mistress of Draebard."

The silence on either side of me spoke volumes, and I did not dare look at either of my companions. I could imagine their expressions of shock all too clearly as it was. Indeed, even Magoldis' impassive expression finally slipped, revealing keen interest.

I knew my features were plain and my body, angular and boyish. It was what had allowed me to pass for male these last three years. Still, I could tell from the Leader's face that she was looking past all that and seeing the feminine attributes underneath. It was all I could do not to tremble as the unimaginable consequences of what I had just done began to clamor for my attention.

"Well. That is certainly unexpected," Magoldis said. "I've never met a female Horse Master before. To find one from Draebard, of all places, is a surprise indeed. I can't help noticing that you have taken pains to look like a man, though."

"Skirts are impractical for starting colts and mucking out pens," I said, forcing my voice to stay matter-of-fact, almost dismissive. "And braiding up long hair takes time that can better be spent doing my job."

Magoldis let out a startled bark of laughter at the last part, and I couldn't help noticing her own waist-length, intricately braided red hair. Sensing I had gained something of an advantage, I pressed on before she could remember that she didn't like us.

"I understand it's traditional for visiting horse tamers to demonstrate their skills," I said. "If you have a suitable horse on hand, I would be happy to do so."

The Leader looked at us speculatively. "I'm sure something can be arranged. Why don't the three of you relax for a few hours? I'll send for you after lunch."

Andoc had apparently found his voice again. "Whatever suits you, Leader. We are, of course, at your disposal."

All three of us bowed and took our leave, passing the dour guards on the way out and heading back in the general direction of Harinel's rooming house. The silence between us was complete, and—to me, at least—more than a little disconcerting. Of *course*, the one time I could have actually used some of Andoc's shallow banter and teasing, the man had absolutely nothing to say.

That changed as soon as the door to our rented room closed behind us and he rounded on me.

"That was simultaneously the most brilliant and idiotic thing I've ever witnessed in my life," he said. I couldn't read his expression as he stared at me, but his eyes were wide and a bit manic.

"Thanks…?" I offered in a small voice, my own mind whirling like a tempest as the full realization of what I'd just done began to truly sink in.

Perhaps sensing that I was frozen in place like a statue, Senovo took me by the elbow and steered me toward the bed I had used last night, urging me to sit. He then sat across from me on the edge of the other bed, dipping his head until I was compelled to meet his eyes.

"Carivel," he said, "I know you didn't think it through completely before you spoke, but it's quite possible that you have played the one card that will soften Magoldis toward our cause."

"My name is Cara," I said, apropos of pretty much nothing.

Senovo frowned. "I beg your pardon?"

"My name," I repeated. "My mother didn't name me Carivel. I chose that later because it could be a name for a boy or a girl. She named me Cara."

The priest was still frowning. "Would you... like us to start calling you Cara?" he asked.

"No," I replied, feeling blood buzzing strangely beneath the skin of my fingers and toes. The edges of the room were starting to take on a grayish tinge. "Not really. I'm sorry—I don't even know why I said that."

"She's in shock," Andoc said from somewhere behind me. There was a sound of footsteps on the flagstone floor and a bit of rummaging. A wineskin appeared in my field of vision. Andoc handed it to me and said, "Drink."

I did. The burn of strong alcohol made me cough, and my vision cleared a little.

"Shit," I said, letting him take the skin away. "What have I done? I just—*shit*."

I looked up at Andoc with a panicked expression, and he could only shrug his agreement. "That's pretty much the size of it, yes."

"I think there's a way this could be turned to all of our advantages," Senovo said from his perch on the other bed. "I need a little time to think about how it could work, though. Right now, I'm more concerned about whether you are in any condition to tame a Mereni horse in a few hours, Carivel."

What? Oh, yes. I'd told Magoldis that I'd do that, hadn't I?

"I'm not sure I want to know what qualifies as a problem horse among the Mereni," Andoc said, oh-so-helpfully. "From what I've heard, even the good ones will take your face off if you look at them the wrong way."

"A horse is a horse," I said, still focused on how badly I'd just sabotaged my life. "All of their problems come from people. It'll be fine."

"Even so," Senovo said, "you should probably rest first."

I almost laughed out loud at him, but stifled it at the last moment so it came out as more of a choking noise. "Sure," I said. "Rest. I'll get right on that."

"Hey," Andoc said. I felt a jolt of surprise when his callused fingers framed my chin and tilted my face up until I was forced to look at him. "If Senovo says there's a way for this to work out, then you can believe him. We just need to keep you from getting eaten by a fire-breathing Mereni dragon-horse before then. I need to know that you're taking this demonstration seriously, and can handle it."

A small thread of anger pierced the gray blanket of despair cloaking my thoughts, which was perhaps the best thing the irritating sod could possibly have done for me at that moment.

"Of course I can handle it," I snapped, jerking my chin free. "Do you think I got my position as Jorun's assistant on the basis of my fine singing voice, Andoc? Or perhaps my talent as a dancer? Don't you dare patronize me!"

Andoc let out a breath, as if with relief. "That's better," he said nonsensically.

"Who's the First Warrior of the Mereni these days?" Senovo asked. "Because you'll probably be fighting him later this afternoon, Andoc."

"I have no idea," said the warrior. "I'm sure I can give him a run for his money, though. Do you know the High Priest here?"

"Only by reputation," Senovo said. "They say he has the second sight. I think he and Rhystel know each other personally."

The mention of the injured High Priest dampened our already strained spirits further. After a moment, Andoc sighed gustily and said, "Come on, both of you. I'm tired of playing fetch and carry with your food. Let's go take a look around the village. We'll get something to eat before people start throwing man-eating horses at you, Carivel, and trying to poke me with sharp objects. And... well... whatever it is they're likely to do to you, Senovo."

"I shudder to think," Senovo said. "It will probably involve mind-altering substances and copious amounts of chanting, though."

"I think you're getting the best end of this deal, my friend," Andoc said, and I couldn't help but agree. Something a bit more strongly mind-altering than the wine Andoc had given me earlier sounded absolutely wonderful right about now.

⚜

Andoc chivvied us out of our rented room and toward the nearest stall selling food. Once we'd secured our meals and found a pleasant, shady place to sit and eat, I turned to him, scowling.

"You should have warned me ahead of time that the Mereni Leader was a woman," I said.

"Yes. Sorry about that," he said. "It seemed like quite a witty joke on my part at the time. Not so much, now."

Andoc was extremely lucky that my shock was stronger than my anger at this particular moment. Rather than waste breath berating him, I focused on trying to understand the circumstances we were dealing with.

"So, I gather that's why no one in Draebard even wants to talk about the Mereni?" I asked.

"Partly," Senovo said. "Magoldis was the wife of the last Leader. When he died during a raid on the village, they say she picked up his sword and hacked the attacking Chief to pieces. Afterward, she just sort of... took things over, and the Mereni followed her. That's why she calls herself a Leader instead of a Chief — she claims she'll only hold the position as long as the Mereni choose to follow her."

Andoc took up the thread of the story. "When Volya heard she'd taken over the leadership, he immediately made overtures of marriage, even though the two of them barely knew each other. He'd lost his wife a few years before, and he probably saw it as a way to consolidate power in the region. Magoldis apparently *didn't* see it that way, however. She not only refused him; she basically laughed in his face. It insulted Volya badly enough that he started flying off the handle if he so much as overheard someone discussing it. Before long, the whole thing just sort of became *that incident with the Mereni of which we do not speak.*"

"When did all this happen, anyway?" I asked. "It must have been before I came to Draebard."

"It was," Senovo said. "I believe it was almost five years ago, now."

We ate in silence after that, as I digested what I'd learned and tried not to panic over what I'd done. Afterward, we took in the sights, wandering aimlessly through the unfamiliar village. When we returned, the little messenger girl was waiting for us at the entrance to our room.

"Come to the horse pens," she said in a high, piping voice. "Leader Magoldis says they're ready for you."

I nodded my understanding and the girl hurried off to her next errand. Andoc and Senovo were looking at me with matching worried expressions, and my irritation flared once more.

"I need a straight tree branch roughly the span of my outstretched arms," I told them. "Something strong and flexible, but light enough that I can hold it in one hand. There's probably a suitable one near the pen out back; there are several trees there."

Senovo nodded and left to get a branch for me, leaving Andoc watching as I rummaged through our saddlebags for a piece of cloth. I couldn't find anything light enough for my purpose, so I untucked my linen undershirt and ripped a strip from the bottom edge.

"What are you doing?" Andoc asked, still looking at me like he was concerned I'd gone mad.

"You just worry about poking people with swords," I growled, "and leave the horse stuff to me."

When Senovo returned with a sturdy branch a little shorter than I was tall, I nodded my thanks and tied the strip of linen to the narrow end, anchoring it by twisting and knotting it around a fork in the wood where a twig had snapped off. I grabbed a spare halter and lead line made of light rope from my bag and gestured for the others to follow me. They did, throwing each other a look I couldn't interpret.

The horse pens were at the south edge of the village. We'd passed by them earlier when we were exploring the place. I was somewhat surprised to see the size of the crowd that had gathered there, but I suppose something like this would be a rather unusual occurrence in Meren. Apparently, we were to be entertainment for the town folk as well as emissaries to the Leader.

Magoldis herself was already present. She gestured us forward when she saw us.

"Is there anything in particular you need, Horse Mistress of Draebard?" she asked.

I looked around. "I would like to use that pen, Leader Magoldis," I said, pointing toward a training ring with a high, sturdy fence, about twenty-five or thirty strides across at its widest point.

"Very well," she said. "I will have the stallion brought there and released."

"What's wrong with this horse, exactly?" Andoc asked. "What problem does he have that needs fixing?"

"He maims people," Magoldis said matter-of-factly. "Sometimes he kills them. A pity, since he is otherwise an exceptional specimen."

Before Andoc could do more than go pale and open his mouth to protest, there was a loud squeal from the direction of the other pens. Two men appeared, each holding tightly to a thick rope attached to the tall, muscular black stallion between them. The horse shook its head angrily, trying to lunge for first one man, then the other, only to be yanked back at every attempt. He was easily the tallest horse I had ever seen, towering over little Kekenu by four hands or more.

Magoldis was right—he was utterly stunning. Already, I was plotting to trade for Mereni horses to interbreed with our own stocky mares.

My thoughts were interrupted by Magoldis shouting instructions to the burly handlers, who guided the frustrated, furious animal to the pen I had indicated, fighting for every step of progress. Grabbing the rope halter and my tree branch with its little cloth flag flapping from the end, I hurried away from my appalled companions, wanting to be inside the pen myself before the stallion was released.

"Carivel!" Andoc called after me, and I might have been touched by the worry in his voice if I weren't so irked by it.

I slipped through the rails of the fence on the opposite side of the circular pen from the gate and draped the rope halter over the nearest post for later. Around me, I was aware of the crowd gathering outside the fence, with Magoldis, Senovo, and Andoc right at the front. A nervous-looking boy opened the gate, and the handlers dragged the stallion into the pen. The two men wrestled the animal around to face the gate again. The lad swung it closed until there was only enough space for a man to slip out. The first handler unhooked his rope from the stallion's halter and darted through the opening. The second handler blocked the horse's attempt to bite him with a vicious punch to the animal's tender muzzle and ducked out as well, leaving the remaining lead rope hanging free from the halter. The boy slammed the gate shut and latched it closed, scurrying back out of range.

There was a moment of complete silence as the stallion paced back and forth in front of the gate, the loose length of rope dragging on the ground. I leaned against the fence on the opposite side of the pen, watching from the corner of my eye, my stick held loosely in my right hand, the cloth flag resting on the ground. I had been aware of Andoc's gritted teeth as he stood a few feet away on the outside of the pen… of Senovo's hand on his forearm, holding him back from doing or saying anything rash, but now everything outside of the fence fell away.

The horse shoved at the wooden gate with his nose, making the wood creak, but the latch didn't give. Frustrated, he reared and stomped down with his forefeet, shaking his head and making the loose rope flap around his legs. The stallion turned, acknowledging me for the first time with an explosive snort. Most horses would have threatened and bluffed first before truly coming after a human with the intent to injure, but given this stallion's description, I was not particularly surprised when he pinned his ears and lunged across the pen toward me almost immediately.

I could hear the collective intake of breath from the crowd as he covered the distance in three strides and reared, hooves flailing toward my head. Without moving from my position leaning against the fence, I whipped the branch up and shook the linen cloth in the horse's face, letting it flap against his eyes and ears. Taken completely by surprise, the black horse twisted in midair and nearly fell as he tried to scramble away. Ears flat against his head, he ran back to the gate and shoved at it again, half-rearing this time to crash against it with his shoulder.

I hoped for the sake of the people milling around outside that the Mereni constructed strong gate latches.

After a few moments of ignoring me in favor of testing the strength of the fence, the stallion turned and lunged for me a second time, only to pull up short when I casually raised the cloth flag toward his head and shook it. Rather than rear and strike, he whirled and kicked out at the flapping rag, raising another gasp from the crowd even though his heels didn't come within an arm-span of my body.

This time, rather than return straight to the gate, the stallion galloped along the fence, circling the pen with the loose rope dragging and flopping along beside him. As he approached the spot where I was lounging against a post, I pushed myself upright and took a step away from the fence, claiming a slightly larger area of the pen as my own. The flapping cloth flag forced the animal to skid to a halt and pivot over his haunches, running back in the direction he came. We repeated the same dance a few more times until the stallion no longer gave the impression that he would prefer to trample straight over the top of me as he approached the little patch of fence I had staked out as my territory, instead turning smoothly to run in the other direction.

Once I was confident that we both understood and accepted the basic rules of the game—don't barge into my space or I'll shake a scary flapping thing at your head—I walked to the center of the circular pen, keeping the cloth flag low and unthreatening. Without my presence blocking his way, the horse cantered along the fence in a continuous circle, tossing his head occasionally and striking out with his front feet in mid-stride to express his frustration.

Without letting my attention waver from the large animal circling me, I addressed the crowd, trying to pitch my voice so as many as possible of them could hear. "Basically, between the two of us inside this pen, the one who moves their feet the most loses the game. It's how horses interact with each other, and it's how I'm going to interact with him. The dominant horse — me, in this case — stands by her pile of feed, and if another horse tries to come up and displace her, she just pins her ears back and snaps her teeth, or maybe cocks a hind leg as if to kick. The other horse skitters away, out of reach, and the dominant horse keeps her pile of hay."

I lifted the stick I was holding ever so slightly. "This stick is how I pin my ears back and threaten to kick. It doesn't hurt him, but he doesn't want it flapping near his face because it's unfamiliar and frightening. As long as I only use it to give clear and reasonable instructions about how he should act around me, it can be the key to letting us build a rapport without anyone getting hurt."

I could hear some muttering from the crowd in response to my words, but my eyes were only for the animal circling me. As he passed the gate, I smoothly moved forward toward the fence at an angle, once again blocking his progress, forcing him to turn into the fence and change directions.

Every second or third time the stallion circled past the gate, I repeated the exercise. Gradually, the horse slowed to a trot, the turns becoming smoother and his expression calmer. In addition to turning into the fence to change direction, I coaxed him into turning toward me before swerving back out to go the opposite way, flapping the cloth at him whenever he laid his ears back or tried to crowd in toward the center where I was standing. When I could reliably turn him inward and outward, speed him up with a flick of the flag toward his haunches, and slow him down with a flick toward his nose, I took a deep breath and let it out, lowering the stick and fading backward a few steps.

The black horse turned in toward me in anticipation of another change of direction, but slowed to a stop when I did not raise the flag or step toward him to push him back out toward the fence. We watched each other for a long moment before old habits returned, the stallion pinning his ears and pressing forward. Rather than allow him to build up to a full-blown charge, I stepped forward as well, the flag raised slightly in warning. Instead of turning tail this time, he scrambled backward a couple of steps and stopped, still facing me. I relaxed, letting him know that was all I wanted, and he blew out a soft breath, licking and chewing thoughtfully as he pondered this strange new development in his life.

"Now that he respects my little cloth flag and stick, it's time to teach him to accept it without fear," I told the crowd. "Fear of the flapping cloth kept him at a safe distance from me in the beginning, but fear will be dangerous now that I'm ready to approach him. Trust will serve me better for that."

Keeping my body language friendly and relaxed, I began to lift the flag smoothly toward the horse's body, withdrawing it and taking the pressure off whenever he showed signs of acceptance. Any hint of aggression was met with a quick flap as a reminder of who was in charge of our nascent partnership.

Within half an hour, I was able to run the cloth softly over the stallion's neck and shoulders, using the stick as an extension of my arm. When he stood quietly with his head lowered and his eyes soft, I untied the cloth from the stick and laid the stick aside. With the cloth in my hand, I continued to stroke it over the front half of his body, letting my fingers brush against his sleek coat occasionally. Before long, I was running my right hand over him directly, the cloth wadded up in my left in case he decided to revert to aggressive behavior.

He didn't.

Moving slowly and deliberately, I unfastened the stiff, heavy leather halter from the stallion's head. Gods knew the last time it had been taken off—the hair underneath was worn away and the exposed skin was rough and scabby. The horse closed his eyes and released a quiet sigh, as if of relief. I let my fingers rub delicately over the damaged flesh, scratching lightly when he pressed against me, rubbing to relieve an itch. We stayed like that for several minutes.

With a final stroke, I straightened his forelock and took a step back. The stallion raised his head, watching me with pricked ears. I turned my back on him and calmly walked toward the far side of the pen, where my soft rope halter was still hanging from a post. Behind me, I heard the horse follow quietly, his hoof beats muffled by the sandy soil of the pen. There was yet another noise of surprise from the crowd, followed by excited murmuring as I picked up my light rope halter and let the stallion sniff at it curiously. When he was satisfied, I placed it around his head and adjusted the knots until it wasn't resting over any of the sores left by his old halter.

Using the cloth flag to communicate and reinforce my requests, I ran through some simple exercises to get him yielding to the rope, pleasantly surprised to find that when he wasn't being dragged around by two burly men, he was actually fairly light and responsive. Once I was satisfied with my ability to lead him safely, I approached the place where Magoldis was standing, flanked by Andoc and Senovo, both of whom looked like a stiff wind might blow them over at any moment.

"Leader Magoldis," I said, "if you are satisfied, I feel this is a good place to end the day's session. Where is the horse normally penned? I'll take him there and save his regular handlers the bother."

Magoldis had a smile playing around her lips that looked like it wanted to be a full-blown grin. She turned to a middle-aged man standing a short distance away, raising an eyebrow in question. By the man's sour expression, I guessed him to be the Mereni Horse Master. Going on what I had seen so far, I couldn't say that I was particularly impressed.

"We keep him in the southernmost corral," the man said gruffly. "Best wait until the crowd leaves, though. He'll start acting up again once he's out of that training pen."

Magoldis looked to me, one eyebrow quirked and amusement still written on her face.

"He's fine," I said in response to the unspoken query. "If he decides to test the boundaries, I've still got this." I flashed the little cloth rag, still crumpled in my hand. Beside me, the black horse shook his head and sneezed, spraying everyone around with a fine mist of snot.

The Leader laughed aloud, obviously delighted with the afternoon's entertainment. "Off with you then, Horse Mistress Carivel of Draebard. I think you've taught us all a thing or two today, not just the horse."

Upon hearing the title of *Horse Mistress*, pleasure and panic washed over me in roughly equal measure. Beside me, the black horse stepped sideways, tossing his head nervously, and I forced myself to let the conflicted feelings slide away for the time being. "It was my pleasure," I said. "I should warn you, though, if this horse continues to get the same sort of treatment he's always gotten, he will revert to his old ways in no time at all."

The Mereni Horse Master's sardonic snort did not escape me, but Magoldis only said, "That would be true of any living creature, I think. Not to worry, I've had a thought on that subject. We'll discuss it later."

She gestured for me to take the horse back to its pen, so I gave a short bow and did so. The stallion fussed a bit once we were in the open, but subsided quickly enough when I backed him up several paces, flicking the cloth back and forth toward his chest until his attention was firmly focused on me once more. I released him into his corral, daring anyone to comment as I removed the light rope halter, leaving him free and bare headed for the first time in who-knew-how-long.

Nobody said a word.

The crowd was dispersing, sensing that the afternoon's drama had drawn to a close. When I returned to the training pen to retrieve my stick, however, Senovo and Andoc were waiting for me. Andoc, still looking a bit wide-eyed, hustled me away to a private spot around the corner from one of the horse sheds.

"What—?" I began, only to be wrapped in an enthusiastic embrace strong enough to lift my feet off the ground and drive an undignified squeak from my lips.

"That was amazing," Andoc said in my ear. "You were amazing. Why didn't you tell us earlier how amazing you are?"

The blush that reddened my skin was from more than just embarrassment as Andoc's scent of musk and sweat surrounded me, his breath tickling my neck. Flustered, I pushed him back to arm's length and said, "Andoc, this is just what I *do*. It's my job!"

Senovo's voice came from behind me, and I twisted until I could see him. "Nonetheless, it *was* a rather extraordinary spectacle," he said.

I shook my head, bewildered. "Not really. The horses with the most extreme behavior problems are generally the ones that are most desperate for someone to trust."

Senovo's lazy green eyes crinkled at the corners in the most genuine smile I had seen from him since before the attack on Draebard. "Who knew there was such wisdom to be found in the horse pens?" he asked. "Happily, as payment for that bit of insight into the soul of man and beast, I believe I can offer you a workable plan for your present precarious situation, along with a backup plan, should that fail."

I stared, looking back and forth between Senovo and Andoc.

"Really?" I asked, feeling the first stirrings of hope.

"The first plan is entirely dependent upon Leader Magoldis' willingness to throw in her lot with ours against the Alyrions," Senovo cautioned. "If she does, however—and she appears to be particularly well inclined toward you at the moment—Volya may be desperate enough for her help that he would be forced to acknowledge you as a female, and Draebard's Horse Mistress. It would need to be implied that Magoldis' willingness to offer her troops hinged upon his acceptance of a female into a male role, as proof that he has changed in the years since his ill-received marriage proposal and attempt to usurp her position. Besides, Volya is a practical man. After three years, he can hardly argue that your presence in the horse pens constitutes any real threat to the herd, can he?"

I was struck speechless at the audacity of the suggestion. What Senovo was describing was essentially blackmail. Blackmail *of the most powerful man in the village.*

"And if it doesn't work," Andoc added, "I think I can safely say that you could find a place here in Meren if you had to. Although it doesn't look like you'd be too popular with the current Horse Master, unfortunately."

It was almost too much for me to take in. "I don't know what to say," I whispered faintly. "I'll... I'll have to think about it. But, Senovo? Andoc? *Thank you.*"

Senovo shrugged it off. "As I said, much of it depends upon Magoldis. You mustn't think your situation hopeless, though. It's not."

I nodded, still stuck for words.

"Now," Senovo continued, "we should probably head back to the central square. I believe it's Andoc's turn to attempt to curry favor."

"You'll be fighting?" I asked, turning back to the warrior.

Andoc cleared his throat, looking strangely discomfited. "Yes, that's right."

I frowned, looking to Senovo for answers. The look of sly amusement had returned to the eunuch's face.

"Indeed. Andoc will be facing Varanis, First Warrior of the Mereni," he said.

NINE

My mind was blank for a moment. When the name finally registered, a ridiculous smile spread slowly across my face. "Varanis? As in, the guard outside the meeting hall? Andoc, you're fighting a woman?"

"More specifically, I'll be fighting Magoldis' firstborn daughter," Andoc said, looking like he'd eaten something sour. "If I accidentally hurt her, they'll probably have me publicly flogged. This is going to be a nightmare."

I couldn't help it. I collapsed into laughter as Andoc glared at me, his offended expression sending me into further uncontrollable fits that had as much to do with a release of the day's tension as it did with Andoc's situation.

"If you're *quite* finished," he grumbled when I had finally wrested myself back under control, wiping tears from my eyes as Senovo looked on tolerantly.

"Oh, yes," I said. "I'm definitely finished. Come on; let's hurry back to the village center. This is going to be the highlight of the entire journey for me."

Andoc merely growled something unintelligible in response.

The crowd in the village square was even larger than the one at the horse pens had been. Apparently, word had spread that the visitors from Draebard brought good entertainment value with them. Andoc retired briefly to our room to prepare himself for the fight, which Senovo reassured me was not actually intended to result in death or serious injury. Or in public flogging, for that matter.

Still, I could see that it was a bit of a delicate situation. Andoc obviously thought that his victory was a foregone conclusion. And, indeed, he was a highly respected warrior for a reason—he was good. *Very* good. If the fight were completely one-sided, Magoldis might be offended at seeing her daughter humiliated. However, to be seen to purposely fight with less than one's full skill would be dishonorable in the extreme, and also highly insulting.

By comparison, I'd had it easy—no one was rooting openly for the horse. Well... except, possibly, for the Mereni Horse Master. Senovo gained my attention with a touch to my elbow and indicated that we should join Magoldis at the front of the gathering spectators.

"We'll be expected to attend the Leader during the contest," he explained, and I nodded my understanding.

A platform had been erected at one end of the square, with three heavy wooden chairs placed atop it. Magoldis sat in the middle chair, looking down over an empty stretch of packed dirt where the fight would presumably take place. When she noticed us, the Leader beckoned us forward and onto the platform.

"Sit," she said, indicating the other two chairs with a flick of her hand. Senovo bowed and lowered himself into the chair at Magoldis' left with a graceful swish of robes. I quickly followed suit, sitting on her right.

A chalk circle perhaps half the size of the training pen I'd used earlier had been laid out before us on the hard ground. I was familiar with this sort of contest—it was a common enough occurrence both in Draebard and the village where I'd grown up whenever the warriors got too bored between skirmishes. The opponents would battle either to first blood, capitulation, or until one of them was driven out of the circle. Such competitions were generally friendly enough within the ranks of a village's warriors; I had a sneaking suspicion they would be less so between warriors from different tribes. Especially tribes with as much bad blood between them as the Mereni and Draebardi.

In contrast to the hush that had characterized the spectators around the horse pens, the crowd around the village square was raucous and celebratory. Mereni warriors were making their way toward the front, forming the first rank around the fighting circle. I had no doubt they would provide as much distraction for Andoc as possible during the contest.

I fidgeted slightly in my seat, resisting the urge to look to Senovo for… what? Reassurance? Calm? Cheers erupted from the far end of the square, spreading among the crowd until the noise became nearly deafening. The spectators parted, opening a path for Varanis to approach. Magoldis' daughter wore leather armor over her shoulders, forearms, and torso. Her bronze shortsword hung at her waist, and in her left hand, she carried a leather-covered wooden shield bearing the Mereni crest of a horse head and a lion head painted back to back. Her fiery hair was plaited tightly against her head and secured with a leather headband.

She entered the chalk ring to chants of "Varanis, Varanis!" and stopped before the platform we were sitting on, saluting the three of us with her sword. Watching Senovo from the corner of my eye, I copied him as he rose and bowed deeply to the First Warrior. When we had seated ourselves once more, Magoldis spoke loudly to the assembled crowd, who quieted immediately.

"Who challenges Varanis, First Warrior of the Mereni, to single combat this day?" she called, her voice carrying across the square.

"I do!" called a voice in response.

The crowd parted once more, this time with jeers and catcalls, though they seemed relatively good-natured to my ear. I couldn't help but catch my breath at the first sight of Andoc as he stalked toward the circle. He was wearing only soft leather boots and the loincloth he used for sparring, but he had tied back his hair and painted his face and body with swirls of red and yellow ochre war paint, as if for a true battle—Volya's colors, and now his as well. In addition to his bronze sword, which was longer and heavier than Varanis', he grasped a cone-shaped bronze buckler in his left hand rather than a full shield. The buckler was smaller and lighter than a shield—maybe half again as wide in diameter as Andoc's spread hand—though it performed roughly the same function. He would use it to protect his hand and arm while blocking blows from Varanis' sword, and perhaps to try to trap her blade during an attack.

It was a surprisingly nuanced approach. In a contest that ended with first blood, showing that much exposed skin was a rather blatant expression of confidence... and yet, the full war paint was a sign of deference and respect to one's opponent. Andoc was armed and dressed for speed and maneuverability over strength, implying that he did not assume he could simply overpower his female opponent. Given that she was taller than him by perhaps half a head, I figured that was probably a wise assumption.

Andoc entered the circle and came to a halt next to Varanis, bowing to Magoldis before raising his sword in salute.

"Andoc, First Warrior of Draebard, challenges Varanis of the Mereni," Magoldis called to the crowd, and was rewarded with a response of hoots and derisive catcalling. When it quieted, she continued, "Andoc. Varanis. Face each other. You will fight until first blood, capitulation, or expulsion from the circle."

The two fighters faced each other, Andoc with a sunny smile and Varanis with a sneer. When they had bowed to each other, Magoldis raised her hands and clapped once, sharply.

The two immediately fell into fighting stances, circling each other warily. Varanis was the first to lunge, her sword knocked to the side by Andoc's buckler even as her shield impacted his shoulder with an audible thump. Andoc twisted, not giving ground, and tried to trip her with an ankle behind her right leg. Varanis staggered back a step but kept her balance, and the two resumed their wary dance near the center of the chalk circle.

Andoc feinted left and pressed right, letting Varanis' blade slide along the buckler until he could trap her sword arm, tangling it with his. Her heavy shield protected her from his longer blade as they grappled. Andoc briefly gained enough leverage to spin them close to the chalk edge of the fighting ring, only to have it nearly come back on him when she threw her weight sideways, forcing him even closer to the edge than she was. He broke free at the last instant, dancing sideways away from both her blade and the chalk line.

Moving faster than I expected, he whirled past, trying to flank her on the right so he could get around her shield. Varanis' sword clanged against his buckler hard enough to make me wince in sympathy, but he wrenched her blade to the outside and swung low with his own sword. In a move so impressive that it made me catch my breath, Varanis leapt over the sweeping cut, Andoc's blade swishing through air where her lower legs had been an instant before. She came down swinging, the shield in her left hand slamming into Andoc's unprotected right side and sending him to the ground.

The crowd roared and my fingers clenched the edge of the chair convulsively, but Andoc rolled to his feet in a single smooth movement, weapons still in hand. He shot Varanis a terse nod of respect, and her responding grin was predatory. The tip of her shortsword described a looping figure of eight as she spun the blade with a loose, easy motion of her wrist.

The pair stepped forward in unison, clashing once more, but rather than parry with the buckler, Andoc met her blade with his own heavier one. Both swords would show dents in the blades from the impact, I was sure, but the tactic left Andoc's metal buckler free to deliver a solid punch to Varanis' left temple. She staggered back from the blow to the sound of the crowd's vocal displeasure, dropping to one knee before quickly righting herself and shaking off the hit.

Andoc didn't allow her time to recover, lunging under her guard and attempting to force her out of the circle. Varanis shouted in surprise, losing her grip on the shield, which fell to the ground and rolled just past the edge of the chalk, out of reach of either fighter. Both warriors wrapped each others' sword arms with their free arms, trapping the blades as Varanis set herself against Andoc's charge. It was a contest of brute strength now, and I looked on avidly as the pair wrestled for the upper hand.

Varanis had the advantage of height, while Andoc had the advantage of muscle. Completely against my will, I found myself thinking about what it would feel like to be trapped in those sinewy arms, wrestled to the ground and pinned there beneath Andoc's hard body. I shifted uncomfortably in my seat, suddenly feeling warm and jittery.

It was obvious that Varanis shared none of my interest in ending up beneath Andoc at the moment, and would probably sympathize more with my frequent desire to do him bodily injury. To that end, she took advantage of the close quarters to head-butt him in the face. Andoc went down with a grunt, but managed to pull the Mereni warrior down with him, their arms and legs tangled together. He used their momentum to roll them over, and had almost succeeded in pinning Varanis, when she kneed him directly in the groin.

There was a collective wince from the male warriors gathered around the circle, who up until that point had been cheering and calling out taunts at the visiting fighter. Andoc curled to the side in reaction, and Varanis wrenched herself free and rolled to her feet. She'd kept hold of her blade as they grappled, and smoothly brought the tip down to rest above Andoc's heart.

For a moment, the only sound was Andoc's harsh breathing as he tried to wrest the sudden agony under control. When he spoke, it still came through in his hoarse voice, if not in his actual words.

"So," he said, grinning up at Varanis through the pain. "We'll call it a draw, then?"

Senovo's huff of amusement was nearly silent, and was quickly swallowed by less restrained laughter from the crowd. Varanis stared down at him, a bruise blossoming on the side of her face from Andoc's metal buckler. Without speaking a word or breaking expression, she flicked her wrist and the tip of her sword drew a thin red line across Andoc's left pectoral. Andoc sighed, and let his head fall back against the packed dirt. Varanis stepped back, and beside me, Magoldis rose from her seat.

"The victory goes to Varanis, First Warrior of the Mereni!" she called, and the crowd erupted into cheers. "A good fight, well matched."

Below us, Varanis sheathed her sword and offered a hand to Andoc, pulling him to his feet when he accepted it. Her tone was arch when she spoke, but the words were accompanied by the first hint of a smile I had seen from the woman. "Hmm... I begin to see why old Volya thought he needed our help."

Andoc's answering smile was wry. "One battle with you at our side, and the Alyrion troops will start wearing codpieces along with the rest of their strange silver armor," he said.

"I trust I haven't permanently deprived the world of offspring from Draebard's First Warrior," Varanis said, speaking under the cover of the crowd's celebration.

"I daresay the likelihood remains as great as it ever was," Andoc replied, and I frowned at his careful wording. "I trust that I, in turn, have not deprived the world of your beauty."

Varanis snorted and prodded gingerly at the bruise on her temple. "I'll probably gain a slew of new suitors based on the story alone," she said.

"In that case," Andoc said with a bow made stiff by the bruising on his side and the pain that was doubtless still plaguing him, "I thank you for a challenging fight. You are a talented warrior, Varanis of Meren."

"And you, a worthy opponent, Andoc of Draebard," Varanis replied, bowing in turn.

Pleasantries completed, Varanis allowed herself to be pulled away by her compatriots, who were evidently intent on celebrating their First's victory by drinking all the wine and ale in the village. Andoc came over to the base of the platform, looking up at Magoldis. A thin trickle of blood trailed down the left side of his chest through the war paint, drawing my eyes.

"Your daughter is fierce and strong, Leader Magoldis," he said. "I would be honored to fight at her side, should the opportunity arise."

"And that opportunity will be discussed in due course, First Warrior," Magoldis said. "You acquitted yourself well despite your defeat. Now, though, you should clean yourself up and present yourselves at the temple in an hour. There is to be a handfasting ceremony tonight, followed by a feast." She turned her attention to Senovo. "The High Priest has requested that you join him in officiating the ceremony, which will be public."

"Of course, Leader," Senovo said. "I will be pleased to assist in any way I can."

⚜

After irritably waving off our questions about his health, Andoc looked down at himself—streaked war paint, blood, and all—and decreed that he would clean up in the river. Like most villages, Meren was built on the banks of a waterway and, like most villages, there was an area on the upstream side where people went to wash.

As the three of us made our way there, we were alternately applauded and jeered by small groups of Mereni going past who recognized us from the day's events. The attention made me blush, but Andoc made a point of saluting or bowing mockingly as the situation demanded. Senovo, unsurprisingly, appeared completely unaffected.

The washing area was fairly empty, since most people were attending the impromptu festival that seemed to have sprung up around our visit. Without ceremony, Andoc shed his boots, weapons, and loincloth before wading in, giving me a shameless view of his well-muscled backside for a few seconds until the water closed over it. When he was chest deep, he ducked under the surface and rose a moment later, scrubbing at his face and hair. He turned back to the shore, wiping water from his eyes.

"Senovo?" he asked. "You need to purify yourself before the ceremony, don't you? Might as well do it here. And Carivel? If you want a dip, it's safe enough. Senovo's distracted by important priestly ponderings right now, and frankly, my balls still hurt like a bastard."

Senovo sighed and threw me a glance that might have contained the barest hint of an eye-roll. Turning away, he unfastened his robes, stripping and wading in after Andoc. Still a coward—always a coward—I called, "I'm good, thanks." Screwing up one tiny iota of courage from someplace deep inside, I added, "I'll just stay here and enjoy the view."

Andoc barked out a laugh, and started scrubbing at his chest. "So, blood and smeared ochre paste get you going, then, Horse Mistress? Good to know."

"What makes you think I wasn't talking about Senovo?" I called back.

"Leave me out of this," Senovo said to both of us, and dove under the water even as Andoc groaned dramatically, clutching the uninjured side of his chest.

"Another wound!" said Andoc, his eyes twinkling. "First the balls, then the breast, and now the heart. What a cruel day to be a warrior!"

I grabbed a pebble from the bank and chucked it at him, successfully bouncing it off his shoulder. Pretending to wince, he laughed again and went back to washing as Senovo surfaced near the center of the river. Keeping half an eye on the two of them, I crouched down by the shallows and rinsed the dust from the training ring off of my face and arms. When the others emerged a few minutes later, clean and glistening, I forced myself to watch openly as they climbed up the sloping bank toward their piles of clothing. I even managed to answer Andoc's challenging leer with a smirk of my own.

We returned to our room long enough for Andoc to change into regular clothes, leaving just enough time to grab some food from one of the many stalls that had been erected around the square before we were due to arrive at the temple. Senovo turned down the skewer of roasted vegetables and chunks of fowl, preferring to fast ahead of the ceremony. He seemed increasingly distant as we approached the ornate temple with its generous courtyard, and I hoped the wolf was not beginning to trouble him as the daylight slanted toward evening.

As we neared the entrance, Senovo took his leave, accompanying two acolytes who appeared to escort him inside to the High Priest. Left alone with Andoc for the moment, I looked up at him, unable to hide the slight twinge of worry plaguing me.

"He'll be all right, won't he?" I asked. "He seems a bit... I don't know..." I trailed off, unsure how to end the sentence.

Andoc smiled. "He's fine. He just takes it very seriously, that's all."

I nodded, reassured. A public handfasting was a fairly significant event, true enough. High Priest Rhystel would have said that to have one on the day of our arrival at Meren was a good omen for the negotiations between our two tribes. In a village this size, there would be many handfastings throughout the spring and summer, but if things were the same here as in Draebard, only a handful would be public.

The priests were always very careful to ensure that both parties were completely comfortable with the idea of coming before the village and sharing their vows and first official coupling with any who wished to attend. Public handfastings were said to bestow luck and fertility on the couple, so it was all too easy for the family of one or the other to put pressure on them to have one. It was the priests' job to be sure it was the couple's own choice, and to guide the ceremony so that both participants found comfort and completion with each other despite the presence of an audience.

I had attended a few such ceremonies over the years for friends or acquaintances. All had been happy events, if somewhat bittersweet for me personally. Such a union had always been out of my reach—or so it had seemed. After Senovo's words this afternoon, though, it was becoming harder and harder not to wonder if such a thing might, after all, be possible some day.

"Come," Andoc said. "We should find Magoldis and join her before the ceremony starts."

With a light touch to the small of my back that was simultaneously settling and unsettling, he guided me into the courtyard. We skirted the stone walls of the temple, keeping to the outer edges of the open area until we saw the Leader's distinctive red hair. She was talking with several elders when we approached, including a short woman with a plait of long, white hair and a face full of laugh lines.

Introducing them to us as the other members of the village's ruling council, Magoldis indicated that they wished to speak with Andoc after the handfasting ceremony about the details of the Alyrion attack on Draebard, and Volya's intended response. Andoc agreed readily, throwing me a look which clearly communicated his relief that we were finally getting someplace with the negotiations.

We were interrupted by the sound of drums and the lighting of torches around the courtyard — clear signals that the ceremony was about to begin. Magoldis led all of us to a set of stone benches with a clear view of the low altar in the center of the open space. We had scarcely seated ourselves when a tall, immensely fat priest appeared from within the shadows of the temple door, followed by the happy couple, naked except for the flowers braided into the girl's hair. Behind them, Senovo followed like a shadow, his hands folded into the wide sleeves of his dun-colored robe.

The little procession emerged fully into the torchlight in the deepening dusk of the cloistered square. I was surprised to see that the man's right arm ended in an ugly stump below the elbow, the flesh red and puckered, but obviously long healed. He was tall and broad, well muscled except for a bit of flabbiness around the belly. A handful of battle scars across his chest and shoulders marked him as a warrior, at least at one time.

"Keenan and Ciero," Magoldis said quietly. "Ciero lost his hand in battle. Now he is an artist of some repute."

I nodded. Beside me, I felt Andoc shudder faintly, and wondered at his reaction.

The young woman — Keenan — was Ciero's opposite in practically every way. She was tiny where he was large, dark where he was pale, and fine-boned where he was broad-featured. She looked up at him with adoration as they approached the altar, and he clutched her right hand in his left as if she were his most precious treasure in all the world.

Meren's High Priest turned to address the onlookers with upraised hands.

"Mighty Naloth, He Who Seeds the Earth and Brings the Rain," he began in a powerful, booming voice. "Bountiful Utarr, She Who Bears Fruit. Bless, tonight, this union between Keenan and Ciero, two of your children. They come before you as they came into this world—naked in the eyes of gods and men."

"*Ever shall it be so*," answered the onlookers in turn.

The High Priest turned his attention to the couple. "Ciero. Keenan. Tonight you tie your destinies together under the gods' watchful gaze. To symbolize this union, Priest Senovo will bind your hands, teaching you to work together as one, relying on each other as you have previously relied only on yourselves. Do you both agree to this public handfasting, freely and joyfully?"

"We do," the pair said in unison, still with eyes only for each other.

Senovo moved from his unobtrusive position behind the altar to face the couple, his back to us. He held out the leather thongs that would seal the handfasting. Keenan and Ciero raised their clasped hands, and Senovo skillfully bound them together palm to palm, weaving the thongs around their fingers so that the ties would last for a night and a day—the prescribed length of time before they could be untied.

When he was finished, he laid a hand on each of their foreheads, murmuring a quiet blessing, and faded back into the shadows once more.

"You are now joined—one heart, one soul," The High Priest intoned. "Celebrate your union before the gods and the people of Meren. Find your joy within each other, that new life may grow from the fertile field of your love."

"Ever shall it be so," intoned the crowd once more.

Keenan's smile was radiant in the firelight as she surged up, standing on tiptoe even as Ciero bent down to kiss her, his abbreviated right arm circling her waist to pull her closer. There was polite applause as the onlookers slapped their thighs lightly, and the drumbeat, which had faded to the background, grew in intensity and complexity—a primal rhythm.

Keenan backed up step by step until the backs of her legs pressed against the edge of the altar, pulling Ciero with her by their bound hands. In Draebard, the altar was covered with the hide of a cow or deer for handfastings, worked into soft suede and used to catch virgin blood, if there was any. Of course, many girls weren't virgins at their handfastings, or were, but didn't bleed. There was nothing wrong with that, but sometimes there was a bit of blood, and in those cases the stained leather was used by the priests in powerful ceremonies.

In Meren, the altar was covered with some sort of soft, woven cloth that appeared to be quilted—stuffed, perhaps, with dried moss or eiderdown. To my eye, it looked considerably more comfortable to lie on than a simple leather hide. Keenan reclined on the stone slab, Ciero following her down as they continued to kiss. Normally, the man would caress his new bride with his free hand until she was near completion before entering her, but Ciero had no free hand and I hoped that Keenan would still be able to find her pleasure without his fingers.

I needn't have worried; pulling back slightly from the kiss, Ciero moved his lips to Keenan's jaw and throat, nibbling his way down to suck at her breasts until she was moaning softly in counterpoint to the drums. He continued down her body, nudging her legs apart to lap at her sex even as her free hand tangled in his sandy hair, stroking and tugging gently in time with her breathy cries. His care and desire for her were obvious, and I felt warmth growing low in my own belly as I watched them. Eventually, Keenan pulled him away, urging him back up the length of her body.

As he loomed over her, I couldn't help noticing how large he was, his erect prick seeming huge in comparison to her tiny body. My mind always seemed to shy away from thinking about how it would feel to be penetrated by a man for the first time, lingering instead on thoughts of what it would be like to have a cock of my own—to thrust into a slick, welcoming space. Now, I winced uncomfortably at the thought of such a large man taking such a small woman, thinking of tender flesh stretching… tearing.

I startled slightly when Andoc's hand rested discreetly on my forearm. "It's all right, Carivel,"

142

he said, his voice pitched for my ears only. "Watch."

Indeed, at that moment Senovo moved forward just enough to murmur a few words to the couple on the altar. Without taking his eyes from Keenan, Ciero nodded and the pair smoothly switched places so that Ciero was the one reclining on his back on the quilted cloth, while Keenan clambered up to straddle his hips. She leaned down, pressing their bound hands over his head as she kissed him and rutted slowly against his hard flesh. When they were both gasping with need against each other's lips, she straightened and guided Ciero's erection into place with her free hand, lowering herself slowly onto it with a cry.

Ciero was trembling, beads of sweat glimmering on his face in the torchlight, but he stayed utterly still as Keenan rocked up and down, taking him a bit deeper each time until he was finally buried to the hilt. They looked at each other in wonder for a long moment before Keenan began to roll her hips, her free hand delving between her own legs to rub in time with the slow thrusts. As she gained confidence, I could see Ciero start pressing up to meet her as she rocked up and down, the two of them moving faster and faster until she tensed with a cry, back arched, eyes clenched shut in ecstasy. Ciero followed a moment later, curling up into her with a hoarse shout, hips losing rhythm.

They collapsed together, breathing hard. Keenan's face was tilted toward us, and I could see her blissful smile as she rested on top of her new husband. His damaged arm came up to cradle her shoulders. I tried to release my emotions with a slow breath through my nose, painfully aware of Andoc's fingers still resting on my forearm. His touch was like a brand. When he removed his hand a moment later, the skin tingled and burned where it had been.

Acolytes appeared at the altar to help the couple unsteadily to their feet and lead them to the room inside the temple where they would spend the remainder of their handfasting together before the bindings were untied. The altar cloth was cleared away and taken inside. In the shadows, I could see the High Priest speaking quietly with Senovo.

Magoldis spoke over the murmuring of the onlookers. "A propitious event, I should say. High Priest Jyrrel is planning a short ceremony next to honor your compatriot, I believe, but if you've no objection, Andoc, the council would like to begin negotiations with you as soon as possible."

Andoc looked surprised, then pleased, before a faint furrow appeared at his brow and he looked at me. Guessing his concern, I nodded and said, "Don't worry, I'll stay here until they're finished. We'll join you as soon as we can."

The furrow smoothed, and he smiled at me. He turned to the others and said, "Thank you, Leader. Elders. I would be honored to accompany you."

Magoldis caught my eye. "We will be at the meeting hall, Horse Mistress Carivel. You and Senovo are, of course, welcome to join us as soon as the ceremony is finished."

"We will come immediately afterward, Leader Magoldis," I assured her. "Thank you for your continued hospitality."

A corner of Magoldis' mouth twitched up in a brief half-smile. "You have proven yourselves to be most diverting guests," she said.

I bowed as the elders filed away behind Andoc and the Mereni leader. When they had departed, I resumed my seat on the bench and looked around. Many people had made their way out of the courtyard at the conclusion of the handfasting, but a surprising number had stayed. Presumably, they hoped to see a bit more of Senovo, who had been largely in the background so far. The drums started up in a new rhythm, and the remaining spectators settled down, their attention returning to the altar, bare now except for two stone goblets.

"Priest Senovo of Draebard," began the Mereni High Priest, "you honor us with your presence and your assistance in the joining of Keenan and Ciero. In return, please accept the honor of our sacred drink, an elixir from the gods which brings truth and clarity to the mind."

I raised an eyebrow. While chanting had been in short supply so far, it looked like the mind-altering substances were finally arriving front and center. I wondered with mild amusement if Senovo was going to be in any condition to attend negotiations tonight.

Senovo went smoothly to his knees in front of the onlookers, bowing his head before looking up at the corpulent High Priest. "I humbly accept the honor of the gods' gift."

Jyrrel lifted both goblets and handed one to Senovo. "Drink with me, then, Senovo of Draebard, that we may both see the truth clearly."

The priests lifted the cups to their lips in unison, Jyrrel standing and Senovo still on his knees before him. For a moment, nothing happened, but then Senovo tensed, scrambling inelegantly to his feet as I frowned in sudden concern.

"No!" cried the slender eunuch, sending my heart pounding against my ribcage as I half rose to my own feet. "What have you—?"

The heavy goblet fell to the ground as Senovo clawed at his throat and chest. I was frozen in place, unable to even breathe as he writhed with panicked eyes, bone and sinew popping and twisting impossibly in the flickering torchlight. A moment later, the light reflected off gray fur and yellow eyes as a large wolf crouched where Senovo had been, snarling with fear and rage as it struggled free of Senovo's robes.

TEN

"Shit!" I choked out as screams and panic erupted around me. "Shit… *shit!*"

High Priest Jyrrel had dropped his own goblet in shock, backing away as the wolf seemed to focus its terror and fury on him. Without conscious thought, I shoved through the bodies running past me and charged forward, sliding to my knees next to the snarling animal and wrapping my arms around its shoulders, heedless of the razor sharp teeth bared inches from my face.

"Senovo!" I said. "You're safe! It's all right, I promise! I won't let anything happen."

The rough-coated, sinewy body in my arms was shaking like a leaf in a storm, so great was the animal's fear. I tugged the wolf backward a bit until our backs were at the altar, feeling it hunker further into the space between my body and the unyielding stone, still growling. New chaos erupted as guards charged into the courtyard armed with swords and javelins, no doubt drawn by the screaming onlookers who had fled moments ago.

The wolf stiffened as the guards' attention honed in on us, its hackles rising under my hands. I tried to press the animal more fully behind my body, but now it was struggling, fighting to free itself from my hold and reach the new threat. I could feel the situation spiraling out of control as the guards raised their weapons. Oh, gods, *where was Andoc?*

As if my thoughts had conjured him, Andoc ran full speed into the courtyard and slid to a halt, taking in the scene with wild eyes.

"*Stop!*" he roared, and shoved past the line of guards to stand between us and them. "Varanis! Have your guards lower their weapons! It's not a real wolf, it's Senovo—he's a shape-shifter!"

I hadn't even realized Varanis was among the guards, so focused had I been on keeping Senovo behind me. Now, though, I recognized the tall, red-haired form as she straightened from her defensive crouch, the bruises from her earlier fight with Andoc livid on the side of her face.

"Will he attack?" Varanis called warily.

"Not if you *lower your damn weapons*," Andoc snapped, still standing squarely between us and the raised javelins.

"Do it," said High Priest Jyrrel, who had retreated to the space in front of the benches. His voice was breathless, but he seemed steadier than he had before as he continued. "This is my fault. I didn't realize… but yes, lower your weapons. Clear the courtyard, calmly and quietly as you can. The situation is under control."

He was looking at me—no, at Senovo—with wonder in his eyes. After a moment's hesitation, Varanis said, "You heard the High Priest. Stand down, and get the remaining people out of here, as quickly and quietly as you can. And Andoc? You *might have mentioned this ahead of time,* for Deresta's sake."

"Not my secret to tell," Andoc said grimly.

Varanis made a noise of disgust, but her guards were already following orders, escorting the remaining handful of frightened spectators away and giving the three of us at the altar a wide berth. I loosened my hold on the wolf's shaggy neck slightly, as it once again tried to cower back behind the protection of my body. When we were alone except for the High Priest, Andoc turned to Jyrrel and said, "We need a room in the temple where we won't be disturbed tonight."

"Of course," Jyrrel said. "Anything you need. There is an empty guest room at the end of the hallway on the left, through that door." He indicated an open doorway off to our right. "I will precede you and make sure the way is clear."

Andoc nodded tightly and crossed the final few steps to us as Jyrrel went to clear the hallway. He fell to his knees and took both of us in his arms, the wolf squirming forward with a whimper to nuzzle between us.

"I shouldn't have left," Andoc said, as I let myself lean on him. "I'm sorry. I should never have left you alone."

At first, I thought he was trembling, but after a moment I realized that it was me. "You couldn't have known," I said into the skin at the juncture of his neck and shoulder, the wolf's fur tickling my left cheek. "It's all right, though. We're all right."

"Thanks to you," Andoc said, kissing first the top of my head, then the top of the wolf's. "*Gods*. They could have killed him."

I shuddered again, and allowed Andoc to help me to my feet. Holding me tight against his left side, with the wolf pressed close against his leg on the right side, he led us into the temple and down the hallway to the room Jyrrel had described. The door had been left invitingly open for us. Inside, there was a low bed with a rough, woven blanket, a table with a couple of candles burning on it, and a chair. There was only a single small window set high in the wall, and once Andoc had closed the door behind us, I finally felt myself start to relax.

The wolf remained glued to Andoc's side as I peeled away and sank into the chair, exhausted beyond measure. Man and beast crossed to the bed together, and I watched as Andoc lifted one edge of the blanket, patting the straw mattress beneath. The wolf jumped up and nosed his way under the rough cloth, circling a couple of times before curling into a miserable ball, completely hidden by the blanket. Andoc sighed and flopped down next to the large lump, which immediately shuffled over a bit to press against his thigh.

Andoc looked up and saw me watching. He shrugged. "It seems to help him," he said. "I think maybe it feels like a den or something. What happened out there?"

I scrubbed a hand over my face, trying to clear the cobwebs. "There were two goblets. Jyrrel and Senovo both drank from them. Jyrrel said the drink was an elixir from the gods. It was supposed to bring truth and... what was it? Clarity, I think. Truth and clarity. A few seconds after he drank it, Senovo started to panic. Scrambled to his feet, dropped the goblet, and then he just... changed."

"Truth and clarity? *Fuck.* I guess it worked," Andoc said, his face grim. "I imagine Jyrrel is running to report to Magoldis even as we speak. There will be no hiding this—not now. He'll have to deal with it whether he wants to or not."

"At least nobody was injured," I said. "Will this hurt the negotiations, do you think?"

Andoc shook his head, smoothing a hand over the tense curve of the wolf's spine through the blanket. "It'll probably help them, ironically enough. Not only did Volya send the likely replacement for the injured High Priest, but oh, by the way, he's a shifter. Even if he never wanted to be one."

"It must be incredibly rare," I said. "It was pretty obvious that no one at the ceremony had ever seen one, and I know I certainly never have."

"It's rare enough," Andoc confirmed, still stroking the tightly curled body beside him. "The High Priest in Draebard before Rhystel was a shifter—he could turn into a ram. And I heard that there was one down south who took the form of a fox. Those are the only two I know of, though."

He looked at the form on the bed, and then to the door.

"You need to get back to the meeting hall, don't you," I said. "Explain about Senovo, and continue with the talks."

"I should, but..." Andoc looked at the wolf again.

"I'll stay with him," I said. "I'm sure he'd rather have you, but we'll be all right. This is too important to risk everything now."

Reluctantly, he nodded and got to his feet. I rose as well. Andoc crossed the small room and pulled me into an embrace. With no defenses left after the day's events, I leaned against his strength and let my own arms close around him in return. I could feel his words rumble through his chest as he spoke.

"I should have been able to prevent all this somehow."

I pulled back enough that I could look up at his face. "Need I remind you that it was my own stupid decision to blab my secret in front of the Leader of the Mereni? I don't recall asking you first. And as for Senovo... well. We'll just have to do whatever we can to support him. Right now, that means you going back there and giving his side of the story, since he can't do it himself. I'll watch over him until you're done."

Andoc nodded, pulling me close again for a moment before letting me go. The wolf had nosed forward until its face was peeking out from under the edge of the blanket. When Andoc walked to the door, it let out a piteous whine.

"It's all right," I said to both of them, crossing to sit on the bed. Andoc, who had paused with his hand on the door handle, nodded again and quickly slipped out. The whine grew into a full-throated howl, and I wondered what the people nearby would make of it.

"Quiet, you poor, pitiful beast," I said over the noise. "He'll be back soon, and until then you'll just have to put up with me. Now shove over — you're taking up the entire bed and I can barely keep my eyes open."

Suiting word to deed, I shoved the animal closer to the wall, the howl tailing off into a surprised yip. Mission accomplished, I reached over and blew out the candles, plunging the room into darkness. After a moment's hesitation, I left all of my clothes on and lay down on top of the blanket. The wolf disappeared back underneath the rough wool, curling up again with a huff. When it had settled, I rolled onto my side, spooning around the shapeless lump and resting my arm across it in a loose embrace. It huffed again and went quiet against me, a warm weight breathing in quiet counterpoint to my own heartbeat.

Within minutes, exhaustion won out over the novelty of the situation, and sleep claimed me.

Light was slanting in through the small window when I was awakened the following morning by thrashing in the bed next to me. The form I was curled around twisted improbably in my arms, and suddenly I was holding Senovo tangled up in the blanket instead of the wolf. The priest struggled free, sucking in great, panicked breaths, and lunged across me to the side of the bed where he heaved and retched, bringing up only a thin stream of bile.

I disentangled us and braced his shoulders before he could slide off the bed completely and land face-first in the mess on the floor. Senovo curled forward, his hands coming up to grasp at his face like claws.

"Senovo," I said sharply. "*Senovo*! It's all right!"

"Oh, gods," he choked. "Gods have mercy on me. Did I—?"

Immediately guessing what he was asking, I shook my head sharply from side to side. "No! It's all right, Senovo. You didn't hurt anyone. Everyone is fine."

He shuddered under my hands, the tremor seeming to rise up from the depths of his body, and his noise of relief was nearly a sob.

"What do you need?" I asked, wishing now that I'd talked to Andoc last night about what to expect. Honestly, I'd assumed he would return before Senovo changed back. Had the negotiations really run all night?

Senovo just shook his head in lieu of an answer, his face still buried in his hands. "Where's Andoc?"

"I sent him back to the meeting hall to continue the talks," I said, adding, "He wanted to stay here."

"You did the right thing," said Senovo, letting his hands slide down to rest limply in his lap. "The elders. Do they... know? About the wolf?"

"I'm afraid the whole village knows by now, Senovo," I said. "I'm truly sorry."

"I'll have to tell Rhystel when we get back," he said in a distant, listless voice. "If he still lives."

"Rhystel loves you like a son," I said. "He'll understand."

It was the wrong thing to say, or maybe the right thing. Senovo curled forward, shoulders shaking as he began to weep silently. I thought of all the tears I had shed for Jorun and the others over the last few days, and wondered if this was the first time Senovo had truly succumbed to his grief.

Unsure what to do, I settled on reaching for the hand nearest to me and twining my fingers with his, squeezing tightly. That was how Andoc found us some time later, when he entered bearing a pitcher of water and a pile of neatly folded clothing and clean rags for washing. His brow furrowed as he took in the scene. He set the items he was carrying on the table and detoured around the small puddle of sick on the floor to sit at Senovo's other side, shoulder to shoulder.

Seeming to draw strength from Andoc's touch, the priest took a deep breath and straightened, staring vacantly across the room.

"I'm deeply sorry, *amadi*," Andoc said. "I betrayed your trust and told the elders parts of your story. It was either that, or let them start speculating wildly about why you hid your ability, and why the wolf was so threatening."

Senovo nodded, eyes still focused on something distant. "It doesn't matter. None of it matters now."

"Are they inclined to help us?" I asked.

"They haven't turned us down outright," Andoc said. "They questioned me all night and into the morning before finally taking a break for food and rest. They'll reconvene this evening to discuss the matter privately between themselves, and then we'll see, I suppose."

"Is anything expected of us today?" I asked.

Andoc shook his head, and I noticed for the first time how tired he looked. "Not as far as I know. I think Magoldis realizes that we need some time to regroup after yesterday."

We were interrupted by a soft tap at the door. "It's Jyrrel," came a muffled voice. "May I enter?"

Andoc and I looked to Senovo, who nodded absently.

"A moment, High Priest," Andoc called. To Senovo, he indicated the pile of clothing on the table and added, "Do you want your robes?"

"It's of no import," Senovo said. "The High Priest has already seen everything of me that there is to see."

Andoc nodded. "Come in," he said, loud enough to be heard through the door.

Jyrrel entered quietly, closing the door behind him. He was silent for a moment as he took in Senovo, still half-tangled in the wool blanket, with Andoc flanking him protectively on one side and me, on the other.

"I had a vision," the High Priest began without preamble, "on the night of your arrival. A vision of a young priest, slender and unassuming, wielding power greater than anyone has seen in a generation. When I met you the following day, I could sense none of that power—only a desire to remain in the shadows, and an undertone of fear... almost dread. I resolved to see if I could learn the truth behind the veil. It was self-serving of me, but I promise you that it was not my intention to harm you or cause you pain."

"There was panic. Chaos," Andoc ground out. "People could have been killed. *He* could have been killed."

"Enough, Andoc," Senovo said quietly, straightening his spine and meeting Jyrrel's eyes. "High Priest Jyrrel, I understand why you did what you did, and hold no grudge against you. I must return to Draebard and confess to my lies of omission, but understand this. I wield no power, nor shall I wield power in the future. What you consider power is in fact a weakness of the highest order, which I must strive every day to overcome."

Jyrrel held Senovo's eyes for a long moment, before looking over all three of us with an assessing gaze. "You are mistaken," he said mildly, "but being mistaken is, of course, your prerogative. You have my deepest apologies for causing you pain."

"It would be best if you left now," Andoc said, his anger under control again, but no less obvious for it.

"As you wish," Jyrrel said. "The room is yours to use as long as you need it. I'm afraid that you will attract a fair amount of attention if you go out into the village right now, Senovo."

Senovo only nodded silently, and Jyrrel let himself out, closing the door behind him. The young priest rose and tugged on his smallclothes, which had been cleaned and neatly folded along with his robes — presumably by the temple acolytes. He was wetting a rag to clean up the congealed puddle by the bed when I shook off my reverie and took it from him.

"Let me," I said. "Rest some more. You still look shattered. Andoc? You, too. You've been up all night. Have you eaten?"

Andoc attempted a smile, but it came out forced. "Isn't that supposed to be my line? But, to answer your question, yes, they fed me."

"I'll go back to Harinel's place and check the horses. I can get us some food for later while I'm out."

Andoc nodded. "Hurry back, Carivel," he said.

I swiped up the mess on the floor and accepted the silver coins Andoc handed me for the food. To my surprise, he did not immediately let go of my hand, but instead used it to draw me into another embrace. Tired of resisting my attraction to him, I returned it, holding tight for a long moment. When we released each other, I sought out Senovo's eyes and he dipped his head briefly in acknowledgement.

Leaving the soiled rag on the floor outside the door for the acolytes to take away, I headed down the hallway to the door that led into the courtyard. It looked completely different in the daylight —

innocent and commonplace. Priests and acolytes were scattered around the space, engaged in menial tasks. Several looked up as I passed through, staring until I met their eyes with a challenging glare of my own that sent them scurrying back to their work.

Outside, in the village proper, I kept my head down and walked purposely down the street to the lodging house. I ignored, as best I could, the whispered conversations that seemed to spring up around me. As I approached the corral behind Harinel's ramshackle house, Kekenu nickered softly, and the other two horses looked up from their piles of hay.

I checked the feed and water, pleased that the boy who worked for Harinel seemed to have taken good care of the animals in our absence. Entering the small pen, I checked them over carefully for injuries or swelling after the long journey here, and took a few minutes to scratch under Kekenu's heavy mane while he rubbed his muzzle against my hip in return.

Our saddlebags were still inside our rented room, where we had left them the previous day. I wasn't keen on dragging all three of the heavy bags back across the village with me, so I dug through them and stuffed a few essentials into one, leaving the others behind for now. Errand completed, I decided to stop by the horse pens before returning to the temple and see how the black stallion was doing. As I walked to the edge of town, I wondered idly how long it took a person to become accustomed to people pointing and talking about you as you passed.

When I reached the horse pens, someone finally plucked up the courage to approach me directly.

"Horse Mistress Carivel?" said a boy, whom I recognized as being the one that had manned the gate of the training pen yesterday when the stallion was first brought in.

"Hello, again," I replied. "I'm sorry, I don't know your name…"

"It's Previn," said the lad eagerly. "I just wanted to say how amazing it was to watch you with Nietre yesterday—that's what we call the stallion. This morning I was putting out his hay and he let me scratch his forehead. He just stood there, calm as you please, and let me do it. Before it was always a race for me to get in and out before he charged me. He tore a chunk out of the last boy's arm, you know. It never did heal right."

I let the flood of words trail off and smiled at the boy. "I'm glad it made a difference for you. A horse like that—he needs to know that you've got a plan, and that you'll treat him fairly and look after him. Otherwise, he thinks he has to look after himself, and he'll do it with teeth and hooves before you can even blink. As soon as you let anger or fear guide your dealings with him, you'll lose his respect."

"I'll remember," Previn said, looking at me with something uncomfortably close to hero worship.

"May I go in and see him?" I asked, wanting to follow up with the stallion as much as possible while I was here.

Previn nodded enthusiastically and led the way over to the pen. The Horse Master wasn't around as far as I could see, but several other people looked up in interest as we passed. The crumpled strip torn from my shirt the previous day was still hanging from the waistband of my leather breeches where I had stuffed it when I left the horse pens. Odd to think of how much had happened since then.

I pulled it free and held it in my closed hand as I entered the stallion's pen. Rather than stalking straight up to him like a predator would, I wandered toward him in a gentle arc. The horse looked up from his pile of hay and snorted. As I approached him from the side, I was pleased to see that he moved his hindquarters away, squaring up to face me. As a further test, I motioned him to back a step or two away from his feed, flashing the cloth rag when he hesitated.

The stallion shook his head and pawed, but gave way, allowing me to step up to the hay and claim it. After giving him a moment to think about things, I invited him forward to join me. He sniffed at my tunic curiously for a few seconds and returned to eating, keeping an eye and an ear cocked in my direction. I ran my hands over him as he ate, keeping the strokes rhythmic and sure. After a few minutes, I again asked him to back away from the hay so I could leave without him getting the idea that he'd run me off somehow.

I was pleased that he seemed to have accepted the idea of ceding power to a human, even if I was skeptical of the Merenis' ability to keep him sweet on the idea after I'd gone. Still, the naked admiration in Previn's eyes as I took my leave and returned to the center of the village gave me hope that he, at least, would take my words to heart.

Not wanting to leave Andoc and Senovo waiting too long, I wasted no time in procuring some food and returning to the temple. I opened the door to the room quietly, not wanting to disturb the pair if they were asleep. The light from the window illuminated the bed, where Andoc was indeed sleeping, curled into Senovo with an arm thrown across his hips. Senovo, however, was awake, sitting propped up against the wall at the head of the bed and running one hand slowly through Andoc's tousled brown hair.

"You should be sleeping, too," I said quietly.

"I'm just thinking," Senovo said, the back of his head resting against the rough wattle and daub of the wall.

"Well, stop thinking for a few minutes and eat something instead," I told him, handing him one of the savory, leaf-wrapped cakes I'd purchased. "You and I both have far too much to think about right now. The reality is, though, that all we can do is go home, confess our sins, and hope for the best. Beyond that, dwelling on things is just a waste of energy."

"More wisdom from the horse pens," Senovo teased quietly, and I was pleased to see the hint of a smile playing around his mouth.

"You'd better believe it," I said.

We ate in comfortable silence, Senovo continuing to soothe Andoc with his free hand as the warrior twisted and muttered in his sleep.

"Is he all right?" I asked finally, putting aside the remains of my meal.

"Just restless," Senovo said. "I think we scared him half to death last night."

I nodded, remembering Andoc's expression when he'd charged into the courtyard to find us surrounded by guards with raised weapons. I also remembered the way he'd stepped in front of those weapons without a second thought, and felt a warm shiver ripple through my chest and down into my belly.

"How much do you remember about what happens when you change?" I asked to distract myself. "You must retain some of it—you knew that I was female because the wolf smelled my moon blood."

"I get flashes," said Senovo. "I remember wanting to attack Jyrrel right after I changed last night. I remember you grabbing me—which was incredibly foolish, by the way. I could have killed you." He cleared his throat and his voice, which had grown soft and faint on the final sentence, strengthened again. "I remember Andoc arriving, and the relief of knowing that he would protect us so I didn't have to."

I nodded. "I felt pretty much the same thing when he showed up, to be honest," I confessed.

Senovo stretched across to place his partially eaten meal on the table near the bed. Andoc moaned as he leaned away, momentarily breaking contact. Straightening and resuming his slow caress across Andoc's scalp, Senovo looked at me frankly.

"You should join us, Carivel," he said, sending my heart into a short, staccato rhythm of surprise. "Just to sleep," he clarified. "You're still exhausted as well. He'll sleep sounder with both of us in his arms."

"I don't want to intrude," I whispered. A bald-faced lie—I wanted few things in life more than to worm my way into their partnership.

Senovo shook his head. "It's obvious to all but the blind that he adores you, and you yearn for him. It serves no one for you to continue to deny yourself."

I pulled my eyes away from Andoc's sleeping face to meet Senovo's gaze. "You must realize by now that it's not only him I want."

Senovo made a small, self-deprecating gesture. "You'll do yourself no favors by becoming romantically entangled with a disgraced eunuch," he said.

An unexpected flash of anger tightened my chest. "And neither of you will do yourselves any favors by becoming entangled with a woman who dresses and acts like a man!" I snapped. "Which is why I've been resisting this all along. If we're going to ride roughshod over convention, we might as well trample it in more than one way."

Senovo let out a long, slightly unsteady breath. "Between the three of us, we're likely to end up being run out of town and forced to wander the wildlands," he said, trying for humor but sounding, in the end, as though he fully expected such a thing to happen.

"Then we end up wandering the wildlands," I said. "I did that for weeks after I ran away from the village where I grew up... did you know that? There are worse things."

"In which case, we have come full circle, and I ask you again to join us on the bed and rest."

Senovo was a stubborn bastard; you had to give him that. Suddenly, I felt exhausted—despite having gotten a surprising amount of sleep last night while curled around the wolf. I was tired of running. Tired of fighting my feelings and desires. Honestly, I could think of nothing I wanted more in that moment than to be in bed with the two of them, huddled close together so no one would fall off. For the life of me, I couldn't remember at this particular point in time why I'd been resisting so hard.

"Fuck this," I said out of nowhere and started pulling off my boots and outer clothes almost angrily. "Fuck every last fucked up part of it."

"Perhaps not until Andoc wakes up and we've had a word with him," Senovo said mildly, but the hint of amusement had returned to his eyes.

I let out an indelicate snort and crawled under the blanket, clad in my smallclothes and linen shirt. Any question about whether Andoc wanted me there was answered immediately... as soon as he felt the mattress dip, he muttered, "Car'vel?" and pulled me into his arms with sleepy, uncoordinated movements. I ended up with my head pillowed on his broad chest, one arm and leg thrown over him.

"*Finally*," he breathed, and dropped into a deeper sleep with a contented murmur.

I glanced up at Senovo, still sitting propped against the wall, and received an arched eyebrow that very clearly said *I told you so* in return. With a deep sigh that felt like it cleared all of the dust and cobwebs from the last few days out of my body, I let my outstretched hand inch closer to the eunuch until my fingers rested on his blanket-covered thigh, just above his knee. I was rewarded a moment later when the hand that had been combing through Andoc's hair moved to stroke my own closely shorn head, sending delicious shivers down the length of my spine.

I drifted like that for a long time, feeling safer and more relaxed than I could remember feeling since childhood, before my father had died and left me to my mother's bitterness and anger. I didn't want to miss a moment of that bone-deep contentment by sleeping. Eventually, though, the soothing movement of fingers trailing over my scalp pulled me down into a sort of peaceful doze where everything was warm and wonderful, and the cares of the wider world beyond our closed door were unimportant.

⊱ ♕ ⊰

When I regained awareness of my surroundings, it was to the rumble of low voices nearby. My cheek was still resting on the warm skin of Andoc's chest, but my neck had developed an uncomfortable kink.

"Mmph," I groaned as I tried to get my leaden limbs to cooperate.

"Well, hello there," Andoc said, looking up at me with a quiet smile as I struggled upright.

"Hello," I replied, my voice soft and raspy with sleep.

"Senovo says you and he had a talk earlier," he said.

I looked across at Senovo, who was still sitting in much the same position as he had been. His expression was calm and gently encouraging.

"Yes," I said, after a moment's hesitation. "We came to the conclusion that we're both going to ruin your life with our various secrets and problems, but since you apparently don't care, there's not much we can do about it and we might as well stop pretending."

Andoc's smile grew wider.

"That might be a *slight* oversimplification..." Senovo said.

"Nonsense," Andoc said. "I think that sums things up quite nicely. Perhaps I'll even forgive you for somehow neglecting to ravish me in my sleep once you finally came to your senses, Carivel. I suppose even uncontrollable lust can be pushed to the wayside after what we've been through in the last couple of days."

"My lust is *not uncontrollable*," I groused, somehow oddly delighted that being in Andoc's bed did not erase his ability to get my back up with a few simple words.

"No?" he asked, and pulled me down for a kiss.

The noise that was startled out of me when our lips touched was completely undignified and embarrassing... and I didn't care one whit. Every ounce of my attention was focused on the sensation of Andoc's cool, chapped lips sliding against my own, growing warm and wet as he deepened the kiss. It was *nothing* like the innocent kiss I'd shared with a hapless young girl when I was thirteen and trying desperately to understand myself.

This—*this*—was every passionate kiss I'd ever seen newly handfasted couples share at the altar... every warmly welcoming kiss I'd seen a returning warrior share with his lover upon being reunited after a battle. Andoc's tongue slid across the seam of my lips, teasing them open and licking deep inside. Desire pooled in my belly, hot and heavy and more urgent than I'd ever felt in my life. When we parted, my gasp was as desperate as if I'd been drowning.

My eyes flickered up to meet Senovo's, unsure what I would find in his expression. His face was hard to read, but I had the sense that he still half-expected the two of us to drop him like a hot stone and run off into the sunset together. Apparently, I wasn't far off the mark, because Andoc followed my gaze and frowned, immediately reaching up to drag Senovo down to his level with a hand on the back of his neck.

"You're being an idiot," he growled when they were forehead to forehead. "I can practically *hear* you thinking ridiculous things. Stop it."

With that, he pulled Senovo down the last inch and sealed their lips together in a biting kiss that made me catch my breath as my cunt throbbed in reaction. Senovo made a noise not markedly different than the one I'd made a few moments ago, and Andoc rolled them both over until he was poised above the eunuch, pressing him down into the bed. I sat up to get a better view as Senovo melted under Andoc's lips and hands, closing his eyes in blissful, heartfelt surrender.

When they parted, Andoc looked over his shoulder at me. "I think you'd better come down here and show Senovo that he's stuck with both of us," he said.

I swallowed, and Andoc relinquished his position as I moved to replace him. Looking down at Senovo, still lying on his back with his eyes closed and his head tipped back trustingly, I felt a sudden nervousness. Andoc had made no secret of his desire for me — for all that I couldn't understand what he saw in my angular, coltish body and plain features. We had bantered about uncontrollable lust, and I hadn't outright denied it; he knew full well of my feelings. Similarly, I'd told Senovo straight out of my desire for him earlier while Andoc was sleeping. Even though — as a eunuch — Senovo did not feel the same sort of physical lust that Andoc or I did, it was obvious that he desired intimacy with Andoc, and gained pleasure from being with him.

But did he really want *my* touch as well?

He was so naturally reserved that I wasn't sure. He hadn't mentioned any objections to the idea, but he hadn't encouraged it either. Before I did anything to the priest lying so vulnerable beneath me, I had to know.

"Senovo," I said softly, letting my fingertips ghost over his cheek. "Look at me."

Those extraordinary gold-green eyes blinked open, gazing up at me.

"Just because you and I both care for Andoc doesn't mean that you automatically want my advances as well," I said, trying to shape my misgivings into words. Andoc rested his hand between my shoulder blades, radiating approval, and I relaxed minutely. "I very much want to kiss you right now, but only if you want to be kissed."

Senovo's face softened to fond affection, making something in my chest swell and break open in response. "Carivel," he said, "you've already seen how Andoc and I fit together. I don't know how you and I will fit together—we'll find that out as we go along. For now, though… yes. Kiss me. It pleases me to hear Andoc bid you to do so, and it pleases me even more that you would stop to ask first."

I was smiling broadly as I closed the distance and touched my lips to Senovo's, trying to take possession of him the way Andoc had done, but painfully aware of my own inexperience. Kissing Senovo was completely different than kissing Andoc. Where Andoc had dominated the kiss from the first instant, Senovo yielded beneath my lips. His hand came up to my touch my face, mirroring the way I cradled his cheek. Before long, I realized that he was quietly and tactfully guiding my movements—not controlling, but suggesting different angles, different techniques.

We explored each other slowly, the kiss gentling until it was almost chaste… or would have been if my breasts hadn't been tingling and my smallclothes damp between my legs. Almost without realizing it, I started to catalog the things that made Senovo relax further into the mattress, or puff out a little breath of appreciation. He liked it when I nipped his bottom lip and worried at it; I loved it when he nuzzled up against the corner of my mouth as if begging for more contact. When we finally parted, I was light-headed with desire and the moisture leaking from between my legs was beginning to drip down my thighs.

"Beautiful," Andoc breathed. His hand, which had remained resting between my shoulder blades, slid down to the small of my back.

Suddenly, all I could focus on was *too many clothes – gods, why are we wearing all these clothes*, but before I could begin to remedy the situation, a knock at the door shattered the moment.

ELEVEN

Andoc growled, and flopped over onto his back. "Who is it?" he called.

"Messenger from the Council of Elders," said a young voice.

"Hang on a minute," Andoc said. "I'll be right there."

I couldn't help my own groan of disappointment.

"*Fuck*," he added, quietly enough not to be heard in the hallway.

"Apparently not," Senovo said, and I could tell that the smug bastard was *laughing* at the two of us — on the inside, at least.

Andoc kissed us both quickly and fiercely. He rolled out of the overcrowded bed and pulled on a shirt and breeches. I followed suit and tossed Senovo his robes. Within moments, we were decent, and Andoc opened the door to the hapless messenger boy.

"What is it?" Andoc asked.

"Your pardon, sir," the boy said. "The council asks that all three of you come to the meeting hall."

"We'll be right there," Andoc said.

The transition from animal lust to fidgety nervousness was abrupt and unsettling. As we walked to the meeting hall, I was uncomfortably aware of the way my thighs slid against each other with every step, gradually becoming sticky as the evidence of my earlier desire slowly dried up.

The people watching us didn't help. If I'd thought I was getting a lot of attention when I'd gone out to get food and check the horses earlier, it was nothing to the excited chattering and looks of fear that Senovo garnered as we made our way into the village square. Andoc and I flanked him protectively, but Senovo's face might as well have been made of stone. He looked neither right nor left, and I cursed the circumstances that had transformed him from the relaxed and trusting lover of a few minutes ago to this stiff, defensive figure.

It was almost a relief to escape the curious, excited villagers by entering the meeting hall—right up until I remembered why we were there. Unlike our first visit, the heavy table in the large meeting room was completely surrounded by men and women, with Magoldis at the head. We entered at the guard's behest and bowed before the assembled Mereni elders.

"Thank you for coming," the Leader said. "We have been discussing your proposal, Andoc, and we have a few more questions for the three of you before we reach a final decision."

"Of course, Leader Magoldis," Andoc replied. "Please ask your questions."

A wizened little man spoke up. "Horse Mistress Carivel. We were quite impressed by your demonstration yesterday. If the council agrees to an alliance with the Draebardi, we would like to foster an exchange of both breeding animals and methods of horse training. Would this be acceptable to you?"

"Sir," I said, "I've been plotting to trade for some of your horses pretty much since I arrived." There was a quiet smattering of laughter around the table. "I'd say that's a more than acceptable provision."

"Very well," Magoldis said. "Priest Senovo. I have been speaking to our High Priest about you, and First Warrior Andoc was also kind enough to fill us in on some details of your background."

Senovo stood tall and stony-faced, not quite looking at the men and women around the table. I saw his throat bob up and down once in a nearly undetectable show of nerves, and ached to be able to somehow go back and undo the previous evening's events.

"We would like assurance that you will, in fact, be returning to Draebard to assume your position as High Priest upon Rhystel's death," Magoldis continued.

"Should High Priest Rhystel succumb to his injuries," Senovo said stiffly, "and should the people of Draebard accept my continued presence after learning of my secret, then I will do my duty. There is, to put it bluntly, no one else left. The only other survivors of the temple massacre are mere boys."

Magoldis tipped her head to the side to confer quietly with a silver-haired woman sitting next to her. After a moment, she straightened. "That is acceptable," she said. "Finally, First Warrior Andoc. The Mereni are involved in a disagreement with the Rhytheeri tribe to the south. Can Meren count on the support of Draebard in the event of an out-and-out conflict?"

"An alliance goes both ways, Leader Magoldis," Andoc said. "Should Meren agree to help Draebard, we would be honor-bound to help Meren in turn."

Magoldis nodded. "Very well. Please wait outside while we make our decision. The guard will show you to a room with refreshments where you may relax."

Relax? Seriously? I did my best not to gape at Magoldis in open-mouthed disbelief, instead following the others' example as they bowed and backed out of the room.

As promised, the silent guard showed us to a small room further inside the building, where a bowl of fruit and a flagon of wine sat on a small table with three cups. Andoc immediately picked up a crisp piece of fruit from the bowl and bit into it, crossing to fall into one of the chairs arrayed around the edges of the room.

"Hmm," he said, looking at the fruit. "That's really good. You should have one."

"I think anything I tried to eat now would come right back up," I said, though I did pour two cups of wine, one of which I pushed into Senovo's unresisting hands. "Drink," I told him.

Taking my own advice, I downed half the cup in one go and flopped down into my own chair. "How long do you think it will take?" I asked.

"Put that many elders in a single room together and they could talk all night," Andoc said. "Hopefully, they got most of that out of their systems earlier, though."

"It sounded as though they were close to a decision," Senovo said, and I was relieved that he was still engaged enough to talk with us given the pressure he must be feeling.

"You're not drinking," I pointed out, and he gave me an ironic little salute with his cup before raising it to his lips.

The silence stretched out for several minutes before Andoc broke it.

"If the Mereni agree to ally with us, I want to ride ahead to Draebard and talk to Chief Volya before you two arrive," he said. "Once I know whether he's going to see sense or not, I can leave you some sort of a signal outside of the village to let you know whether it's safe to come back."

I had successfully taken my own advice about not obsessing over my fate for the better part of a day, but now a sense of deep foreboding reared its head once more.

"Volya won't risk the Mereni alliance over your secret, Carivel," Senovo said, sounding very sure. "Once he hears that Magoldis only agreed because she thought the attitudes toward women were changing in Draebard, he'll have to accept you."

"I agree," Andoc said. "Nor will he turn you away, Senovo, when he finds out you've been a shape-shifter all this time. Still, it makes me feel better to have a plan in place."

"What if Magoldis *doesn't* agree to the treaty?" I asked.

"That's a little more complicated," Andoc said. "On the one hand, there's no reason anyone in Draebard needs to hear about either of your secrets if the Mereni aren't coming back with us. On the other hand, all it would take is one traveler or trader coming in and saying the wrong thing to the wrong person, and you'd be exposed, but without the leverage of the treaty to protect you."

"I'm not sure I could go back to hiding my secret," I said, feeling miserable at the prospect. "Particularly if it also meant having to sneak around in order to be with you two. I think they'll have to be told."

"Well," Andoc said, "in that case, let's hope that the council chooses in our favor. We should know for certain before long."

It had been early evening when we were summoned to the meeting hall. As we waited, dusk descended outside the room's single window, followed by full dark. After lighting the candles on the table, Andoc began to pace while Senovo sat pale and distant in his chair, and I fidgeted. We were unable to keep up even a desultory conversation, each wrapped up in our own worries.

When the guard finally entered and bade us to follow him back to the council room, it was both a relief and the pinnacle of all our concerns, both public and private. Magoldis rose to meet us as we entered, her face giving away nothing.

"After lengthy discussion," she said, "the ruling council of the Mereni have decided to ally themselves with the Draebardi against the incursion of the Alyrion Empire. While our two peoples have had their differences over the years, we are all Eburosi, and it is Eburos itself that is under threat — not merely a single tribe."

It was over. All of the tension bled out of me in a single instant, leaving me light-headed. Senovo was cool and composed beside me, but I did hear Andoc's faint sigh of relief.

"Thank you, Leader Magoldis. Thank you, Elders," he said with heartfelt gratitude. "Like you, I fear the attack on Draebard was only the beginning of something much larger, but perhaps if we work together, we can still prevail." He took a deep breath, and continued. "I would like to propose that I leave for Draebard with a representative from Meren as soon as possible, leaving Senovo and Carivel behind to finalize the details. They can follow on with more comprehensive information about weaponry, numbers, and the timeline for troop movements."

"That seems reasonable," Magoldis agreed, and just like that, Andoc's plan to go ahead and speak with Volya on our behalf was in place. "Now, though, it is late and there is nothing more to be done regarding this matter tonight."

We bowed, and Andoc thanked the council once more.

"Wait," Magoldis said, as we were turning to leave. "I nearly forgot. There is one more thing. I wish to make a personal gift of the black stallion to you, Horse Mistress Carivel. You spoke earlier of your desire to open a horse trade between our tribes, and from what I've seen, you are perhaps the best person available to take on that particular horse."

I was struck dumb until Andoc nudged me unobtrusively. "Thank you," I stammered. "That is an unexpected and most welcome gift. I don't really know what to say."

"*Thank you* will be perfectly adequate, Horse Mistress," Magoldis said with a faint smile tugging up one corner of her mouth for an instant. "We'll discuss more details of our future horse trading agreement tomorrow."

We took our leave again and let the guard escort us to the door of the meeting hall. Outside, it was late enough that the streets were mercifully free of curious onlookers.

"Where do you want to go?" Andoc asked us. "Back to the temple, or to our room at Harinel's place?"

Senovo shrugged his indifference, and I said, "They'll probably expect us to be at the temple. If we go to Harinel's, it might take them a bit longer to find us in the morning."

Andoc raised an eyebrow, the light from the torches flanking the meeting hall door illuminating his predatory smile. "Well, well. I do like the way you think, Horse Mistress Carivel."

"We should go back to the temple first, though," I added. "Some of our things are still there, and there's food left over from what I bought earlier today."

"A reasonable plan," Senovo agreed, and we turned down the road to the temple. Andoc's hand settled at the small of my back, in the same place it had been when the messenger knocked on the door and interrupted us. Desire flared low in my belly, making my breath hitch.

Arriving at the temple, we made quick work of packing our meager belongings and quietly slipping back out. The three of us split the remaining food left over from lunch evenly and ate it as we walked across town to Harinel's ramshackle boarding house. I sent the other two inside, wanting to check the horses again. The two geldings were dozing, lying down on the ground, Kekenu snoring comically with his muzzle mashed into the dirt of the corral. The mare was awake, standing watch between them, and pricked her ears as I approached but did not react otherwise. I checked the water trough and reassured myself that all was well before letting myself into the boarding house and entering our room at the end of the hallway.

The door had been left invitingly open. I closed it behind me, took a deep breath, and let it out slowly. Inside, Senovo was seated on the edge of the bed with one leg tucked underneath himself, while Andoc was sprawled on the floor, lounging against the bed frame with his shoulder pressed up against Senovo's inner thigh.

I stared at them both, so beautiful together in the light from the hearth. "We did it," I breathed, the realization washing over me like a warm wave.

Andoc smiled at me, a slow grin lighting up his face.

"I know," he teased. "I was there, remember?"

"No, but—*we did it*," I reiterated, trying to get the weight of it across.

Andoc laughed aloud. "Are you sure that stallion didn't kick you in the head while our backs were turned?"

"Oh, shut up," I told him, grinning like a loon.

Andoc rose to his feet, smooth as a panther. "Why don't you make me?" he said, still smiling and with a gleam in his eye.

I lunged forward, tackling him to the bed and startling a surprised *oof* from him as Senovo scrambled out of the way.

When I was straddling Andoc's hips, my hands braced on his shoulders, I looked down at him with an insolent tilt of my head.

"So sorry," I apologized. "I guess I just couldn't control myself."

Behind me, Senovo snorted his amusement, making my heart swell even further.

"A regrettable character flaw, if you ask me," Andoc opined from his position on his back. "We'll have to work on that."

Before I could come up with a reply, Andoc was twisting underneath me, rolling us both over with an easy strength that made my heart flutter. Two seconds later, I was the one pinned to the bed, Andoc straddling my waist and holding both my wrists over my head with one large hand. I lay on my back, panting as the glow of affection lighting my chest from within was replaced in an instant with a surge of raw, base need.

Andoc tilted his head up to look at Senovo, who had returned to stand at the edge of the bed and was looking down at both of us with a tolerant gaze. "*Amadi*," Andoc said in a conversational tone, "I believe our Horse Mistress is in need of a lesson. Do you want in on this?"

Senovo tipped his chin down as if considering the matter, and I felt a new flare of arousal at the thought of the two of them discussing me casually while I lay pinned under Andoc's bulk.

"Honestly," Senovo said, "I can think of few distractions more attractive right now than beginning Carivel's remedial education in matters of physical love. Besides—I am, after all, still a priest."

Andoc nodded thoughtfully, not budging an inch as I squirmed beneath him. "That's very true. I mean, you're practically duty-bound at this point."

"Indeed," Senovo agreed.

I bucked my hips, gaining myself precisely nothing. "Stop talking about it and start *doing* it, then!" I growled.

Andoc laughed down at me and rolled off the bed. "Very well, Horse Mistress," he said with a mocking half-bow. "Senovo and I are going to move these two beds together so we've got a bit more room to work. Be naked by the time we're done."

TWELVE

My hands were scrabbling at the ties of my tunic almost before he'd finished speaking. The two each took an end of the other bed, Senovo struggling a bit with his end as they half-carried, half-scooted the heavy mattress and frame across the room. My nervous fingers fumbled with the knot holding my breeches laced shut even as I toed off my soft boots. I was shoving my breeches and smallclothes down my hips as they pushed the second bed up against the one I was currently occupying, and by the time Andoc finished rolling up the spare blanket and jamming it into the space between the two mattresses to close the gap, I had flopped back down, completely naked in the firelight.

"Mmm... yes," Andoc said as he rose and began to remove his own clothing. "Very nice. Senovo, I believe I'd like both of you naked for this."

Senovo immediately started unfastening his robes. The priest ran a critical gaze over Andoc's body as he worked and said, "Before we start, are you fully recovered from your... ahem... *unfortunate injury* during the contest against Varanis?"

My own hands, which had been wandering lazily up and down my body as I watched the two of them, stilled. I had all but forgotten the rather vicious blow that Varanis used to end her fight with Andoc.

"Still a bit tender," Andoc said in reply, not sounding overly concerned. "I probably won't be fucking anyone in the traditional sense tonight, but I'm stiff as a board right now and it doesn't hurt… so I'm going to call it good enough for our purposes."

"Perhaps it's just as well. Traditional intercourse brings with it some complications that we could probably do without for now," Senovo said.

I rolled onto one elbow as Senovo's words penetrated my desire-muddled thoughts. "You mean pregnancy?" I asked, the possibility literally not having crossed my mind until Senovo said something. The idea was a daunting one.

"Yes," Senovo said, as he continued to disrobe. "That's a discussion we will need to have at some point, but perhaps not at this exact moment."

It was a relief not to have to worry about it immediately, so I just nodded my understanding and left the question for another day. Stripped down to his smallclothes, Andoc joined me on the bed and let his hand trail down the side of my neck and over my collarbone, raising gooseflesh in its wake despite the warmth of the fire.

"Still doing all right?" he asked, and I smiled, letting my own fingers trace over the hard muscles of Andoc's chest and stomach, as I had dreamed of doing for so long.

"More than all right," I told him.

Senovo joined us on the bed a moment later, as naked as I was. Andoc leaned over to capture my lips in a brief kiss that left me wanting more, before leaning back against the wall at the head of the bed and easing me against him to rest between his spread legs. I reclined against his body, resting my head on the uninjured side of his chest. I could feel his hot, hard length pressing against my spine through his smallclothes. Senovo crawled across the newly enlarged expanse of mattress on his hands and knees, settling next to my hip. His hand came to rest on my lower leg, sliding slowly up to the top of my thigh and sending pleasant shivers through me.

"Every person is different," he said, "but there are a few things that most people tend to enjoy. The most important thing is to be able to communicate with your lover—"

"Or lovers," Andoc interrupted.

"—or *lovers*," Senovo continued, throwing Andoc a long-suffering look, "about your preferences, and know that they will stop immediately if you don't like something."

I frowned. "But... you and Andoc...?"

"I need to feel as if I'm being overpowered," Senovo said, "for reasons that you and I have already discussed. However, if I were in physical pain or needed to end things for some other reason, I would only have to say *stop* and Andoc would stop instantly."

"That kind of sex is a serious responsibility for the one taking control," Andoc added. "I enjoy it—quite a bit, actually—but it means you can't ever lose yourself completely in the moment, because someone you love is counting on you for their safety."

I lay quietly between them for a moment, relishing the feeling of being protected and watched over as I considered their words.

"The first time I saw you together like that, I thought it was beautiful. Now I think I understand *why* it was beautiful," I said finally.

"All such expressions of love have a beauty to them," Senovo agreed. "The pleasure people can give each other is one of the gods' greatest gifts."

A feeling of sadness washed over me. "One that was stolen from you," I pointed out.

"Not at all," said Andoc. "It might take a bit of a different approach, but later I'll show you how to help me break through our mutual friend's cool reserve."

"Oh, yes?" I said, intrigued. "I look forward to it."

"As do I," Senovo said easily. "Now, though, let us return the focus to you. You told me that you had touched yourself, and once kissed a girl but found the experience lacking. Yes?"

"That's right," I said, feeling a faint blush crawl up my neck.

"So you've never lain with anyone, then? Man or woman?" Andoc asked, his curiosity plain.

I shook my head. "I couldn't. I was a social outcast in the village where I grew up—the girl who wanted to be a boy. And I certainly didn't dare get that close to anyone in Draebard. They would have learned my secret. What about you, though?

Have you ever been with a woman before?" I asked.

"A handful, over the years," he said. "Also a handful of men."

That surprised me, although maybe it shouldn't have. Andoc had already proven that he was not particularly concerned about taboo and convention.

"Well… it sounds like I'm in capable hands, then," I said, giving them both a smile and relaxing back in Andoc's arms.

Andoc huffed out a breath of laughter. "I do believe that was a hint, *amadi*. Perhaps it's time for you to put that eloquent tongue of yours to a different use."

"As you wish," Senovo said, sending my desire spiraling to the fore again.

Andoc's hand slid down to cup my breast, testing its weight. I moaned and pushed into the touch, seeking more contact. Meanwhile, Senovo was rearranging himself to lie between my legs, easing them apart to make room. A moment later, I felt the same soft, meticulously thorough lips I had so enjoyed kissing earlier close over a patch of skin on my inner thigh, tongue flicking out to tease the soft flesh. I choked back the cry that wanted to escape, a new pulse of wetness dripping down from between my thighs.

Senovo's mouth moved higher, suckling at a new patch of skin while Andoc let his callused palm slide over my erect nipple, sending another rush of sensation through me. Senovo continued his slow ascent up my inner thigh until I was shaking with desire, squirming against the arm Andoc wrapped around my stomach to hold me in place, trying to get Senovo to move that last... little... bit... higher...

The flat of Senovo's tongue slid along the seam of my cunt at the same instant Andoc's fingers pinched my aching nipple and rolled it slowly back and forth. I arched from the bed, crying out in shock at the jolt of pleasure that raced between the two points. Senovo's long fingers closed over my hipbones, pressing me back down and holding me in place. His tongue continued to lap at me, slipping a bit deeper inside each time. Writhing against Andoc's lap, I felt him thrust his hips up against me, humming approval as he tweaked and worried at the pebbled tip of my breast.

"Gorgeous," he murmured, as I threw my head back and panted with need.

Senovo was methodical and relentless, driving me higher and higher toward my peak before pulling me away from the cliff, only to press me even closer to the edge moments later. Between them, they pinned me in place, unable to twist either toward or away from the delicious torture of hand and mouth. Dragging his fingers away from my nipple with a final sharp tug, Andoc raised his hand to trace over my throat... my chin. When the rough pads of his fingertips brushed across my lips, I stretched up to draw them into my mouth as I had seen Senovo do when he was bound and helpless two nights ago on this very bed.

With the weight of Andoc's fingers pressing on my tongue, and Senovo's lips wrapped around the little bud of flesh between my legs that made sparks tingle behind my closed eyelids, I finally sobbed my release, hips jerking against Senovo's restraining hands as my pleasure crested in a powerful wave and slowly ebbed.

Senovo gentled his movements, drawing trembling aftershocks from my body, and I continued to suck and lick lazily at Andoc's fingers as he pressed them deep into my mouth and slid them back, over and over in an easy rhythm that made me feel like I was floating. Senovo eased himself away, replacing his mouth with his smooth, soft hands.

My thighs and cunt were drenched after my climax. He dragged his fingertips back and forth through the slippery moisture, avoiding the place where I was still painfully oversensitive. After a few moments, one finger pressed smoothly into my slick passage. I grunted around Andoc's fingers and stiffened in surprise. Both men froze. Andoc slid his fingers out of my mouth, and Senovo remained very still.

"No?" asked the priest.

"Sorry," I said, trying to relax around the intrusion. "I've tried that a few times, but I've never liked it."

The finger slipped out immediately, Senovo's hand moving to rest on my thigh instead. I breathed a sigh of relief and tried to explain.

"It doesn't hurt, really... it's just... I don't know. It's not how I see myself, does that make sense?"

"Ah," Senovo said. "I think I understand. You think of yourself more as a man in this respect, too?"

I nodded. "I suppose that's it. When I daydream about sex, I always picture what it would be like to have a prick. To fuck like men do."

"I can understand that well enough," Andoc put in. "I mean, it *is* pretty amazing."

I reached back and smacked him on the thigh—the only place I could easily reach right now—even as I thanked him silently for his unerring ability to cut through the tension.

"In that case," Senovo said, "let us try something slightly different. Andoc, did you bring grease to mix your war paint?"

"As it happens, I did," Andoc replied. "Saddlebag. Left pocket."

Senovo rose and returned with a small clay jar, which he uncorked and set within easy reach. "I'm going to raise your hips up a bit," he told me.

Andoc eased me down to lie flat on the mattress while Senovo pulled the remaining blanket free from the end of the bed, where I'd shoved it out of the way earlier while getting undressed. He folded it up and rolled it into a tight cylinder, urging me to lift my hips up so he could slide it underneath me.

The new position left me feeling wanton and exposed as Senovo resettled himself between my thighs and Andoc half-reclined onto an elbow next to me so he could watch. His free hand roamed up and down my body, sliding over my breasts and belly.

"The little bud at the front of a woman's slit isn't so different from a man's penis," Senovo said, sliding two slick fingers gently on either side of the delicate flesh, up and down, making me gasp and throw my head back—the sensation just on the right side of too much. "It's very sensitive; it becomes erect when you're excited. The closer you are to release, the more stimulation it can take, but once you climax, all but the lightest hint of a touch becomes too much until you've had time to recover."

"Yours is large for a woman's, Carivel," Andoc said, peering between my legs with obvious curiosity. "It really is like a little cock."

"I thought so, too," Senovo said. "I believe it's the largest I've seen."

"*Gods*," I said, the combination of their words and the slow, delicious drag of Senovo's fingers over my flesh driving me to fresh heights.

"However, there's something else that men do with other men—and with eunuchs—that I'd like to try," Senovo said. "Have you ever touched yourself here?"

Without varying the rhythm of his fingers over my deliciously engorged flesh, he slid a knuckle on his free hand down and back, rubbing it over my rear passage and making me see sparks.

"No," I replied, and it came out as an undignified squeak. I cleared my throat, trying to regain control of my voice. "It never—ah! Never even occurred to me."

"But you sort of wish it had, now?" Andoc teased, tweaking a nipple.

I nodded frantically as Senovo twisted the knuckle and pressed more firmly, merciless in his ministrations. "Uh-*huh*," I said, my voice going up another octave. A trickle of sweat trailed down between my breasts; Andoc twisted around and leaned over me to lap it up, pressing a kiss to each pebbled nipple before he straightened.

With almost no warning, I was teetering on the edge again. Senovo — sadistic bastard that he was — must have sensed it, because he eased off, slowing his movements. I couldn't stop the whine of protest that escaped my throat.

"More," I begged. "*Please*, Senovo…"

"Patience," he said. "This will feel a bit odd. Give yourself a some time to adjust before you decide if you like it or not."

I nodded frantically, desperate for more of his touch. There was a slick smear of cool grease over my opening, warming quickly with my body heat. Senovo began to press with a single finger, moving around the rim of my tightly puckered entrance with small, circular motions. The flesh gave way with a flutter of tense muscles and the tip of his finger slipped inside, meeting a second point of resistance. I held my breath as he continued to rub tiny circles, and eventually his finger slid deeper, disappearing into my body all the way to the third knuckle.

"Breathe," Andoc reminded me, stroking my head, and I emptied my lungs with a gasp. "Try to relax."

I forced myself to breathe, trying not to fight against the intrusion inside my body, but painfully aware of the way my muscles cramped and clenched around it. I was just about to beg Senovo to stop when the priest resumed the slow drag of his fingers across the erect nub of flesh at the top of my slit. Suddenly, the sensation that had been uncomfortable a moment before was the single most amazing thing I had ever felt.

"Mmnh!" I said, grabbing the nearest part of Andoc I could reach, which happened to be his bicep.

"Better now?" he asked.

For some reason, there didn't seem to be enough air in the room for me to answer aloud, but I nodded, my eyes clenched tightly shut. Senovo continued to work me open at the same time he drove me closer and closer to my release.

"*Fuck!*" The curse was punched from my chest when he slipped in a second finger, stretching me even wider. Andoc, who had been teasing my breasts as Senovo slowly drove me mad, leaned down and muffled my moans with a searing kiss, taking effortless possession of my mouth. I gasped for air and he thrust his tongue inside, mimicking the rhythm of Senovo's fingers. Andoc swallowed my sobbing scream as I came, straining up off the bed and clenching around Senovo's fingers, completely overwhelmed by sensation.

It went on long enough that my vision dimmed, leaving me shrouded in shadowy warmth. When I came back to myself, Andoc was still kissing me, gentler now, while Senovo carefully pulled his fingers free. I moaned softly against Andoc's lips, feeling empty where I'd been full a moment before. He reluctantly broke the kiss, running his fingers through my short hair, and Senovo pressed his lips to my inner thigh in wordless apology before rising from the bed. The priest returned a moment later with a damp rag. I was vaguely aware that I'd squirted a truly embarrassing amount of release onto the bed during my climax, and I blushed as Senovo gently cleaned me up with the cool cloth.

Once he'd cleaned his hand as well, he discarded the rag and retuned to the bed, pulling the folded blanket out from under my hips and reclining next to me so that I was bracketed on both sides.

"I think we can call that a successful first lesson," he said.

"I'd say so," said Andoc.

"Mm-hmm," I agreed, still floating.

"In fact, I believe we may have broken her," Andoc said.

I smacked him on the thigh again, though the movement was uncoordinated and weak.

"Shut up," I mumbled. "Lemme rest a minute and then I want to see you two together."

THIRTEEN

"That can be arranged," Senovo said, visibly amused.

"Indeed it can," Andoc agreed. "*Amadi*, how are you tonight? What do you need from us?"

"I am well enough," Senovo said. "The wolf is quiet now, watching things from the background. I would enjoy being of use. Or simply being used, in whatever way the two of you desire. As I said earlier, it sounds like a most agreeable distraction from my worries."

Impossibly, the words stirred a new flutter of desire in my sated, boneless body. With difficulty, I rolled onto an elbow. "I want to see you tied again," I told him. "But not fighting and straining — just quiet, submitting to the ropes while he uses you for his pleasure. Is that... all right? Would you like that?"

Senovo guided me forward with a touch to the cheek and kissed me softly. "I would like that very much."

"Told you she'd have good ideas," Andoc said from my other side, letting his fingers trail down my spine. "In fact, I've got an idea of my own that involves you on your knees in front of me, with your arms tied behind your back while you swallow my cock right down to the root."

I was still facing Senovo, so I saw the nearly imperceptible shiver that worked its way through his body, and the way his eyes darkened, the pupils blown wide. Andoc pressed his lips briefly to the juncture of my neck and shoulder before pushing upright and sliding off the mattress. After tossing the folded blanket onto the floor near the edge of the bed, he cupped a hand under Senovo's chin, guiding the priest off the bed. With an uncompromising hand on his shoulder, Andoc positioned him as promised on his knees, cushioned by the blanket.

Senovo knelt quietly as Andoc went to retrieve some rope. I shifted closer to the edge of the bed, unable to resist the temptation to reach out and stroke Senovo's face and lips. Senovo nipped at my fingertip, his amusement once again shining through the reserved mask.

"Hmm... do I need to muzzle you as well?" Andoc teased, returning with the coils of rope.

Senovo released my finger and looked up at him. "That would make it rather difficult for me to choke myself on your cock, don't you think?" he said, perfectly deadpan.

I couldn't stop a bark of surprised laughter at seeing this new side of the quiet, serious man. Andoc snorted his amusement and knelt behind him, pulling Senovo's arms behind his back and positioning them wrist-to-opposite-elbow. When he had tied them firmly in place, he reached around, pulled Senovo's head to one side, and bit down on the long, elegant line of muscle running from the priest's neck to his shoulder.

Senovo's sharp, indrawn breath of surprise stoked the low burn of desire that had been smoldering in my stomach. He held himself stiffly as Andoc worried and sucked at the skin, as if trying not to react visibly to the assault. When Andoc pulled away, there was a livid mark where his mouth had been, and Senovo sagged for a moment before dragging himself upright once more. I stared at the fresh bruise, feeling the sudden urge to fit my fingers to it and press until Senovo cried out.

Andoc grabbed the second coil of rope while Senovo breathed unsteadily through his nose. He eased Senovo back to sit on his heels, and bound him ankle to thigh on both sides to keep him that way. When Andoc stood and backed away to check his work, the priest was left kneeling with his knees spread, the ropes binding his arms behind him forcing his spine straight.

"This what you had in mind?" Andoc asked me.

I nodded appreciatively, unable to tear my gaze away. "He looks amazing. If I were you, I'd be tempted to keep him tied up like this all the time."

Senovo shivered, and Andoc chuckled. "Hear that, *amadi*? Our Carivel has plans to hide you away as her personal concubine."

"It sounds a much more appealing lifestyle than the one that actually awaits me back in Draebard," Senovo said, evidently having regained his composure. "I can't honestly say I'm averse to the proposal."

"Well, it's always good to have a back-up plan," Andoc said, seating himself on the edge of the bed so that Senovo was positioned between his legs. "Here, come and watch, Carivel. If you're up for it, you can do this to him in a bit, so you'll want to see what's involved."

I wasn't about to miss it—the image of the priest using his mouth on Andoc had been popping up randomly in my thoughts during idle moments ever since I watched Senovo fellating his lover's fingers two nights ago, his face a picture of bliss. I knelt on the bed behind Andoc and rested my chin on his shoulder, wrapping my arms across his chest and looking down at the bound man. Senovo gazed up at us through dark eyelashes, and I couldn't stop the little rumble of appreciation that escaped my throat.

"He is good, isn't he?" Andoc agreed.

"Years of practice," Senovo said, leaning forward to rub his cheek over the tent in Andoc's smallclothes like a cat, never breaking eye contact.

Andoc growled low and grabbed the heavy braid of hair at the back of Senovo's head, using it to force him back. "Enough talk," he said, and began unlacing his smalls with his free hand.

Senovo's eyes glazed over at the manhandling and a small huff of breath escaped his lungs. He licked his lips, completely powerless in Andoc's grasp with his arms and legs bound. I was torn between watching Senovo's face and watching Andoc pull his generous cock free of his smallclothes, my eyes flickering back and forth between the two.

Andoc was not as large as Ciero had been, a fact for which I was frankly rather grateful. Nonetheless, his prick was thick and hard, and I could hardly wait for a chance to explore it. Now, though, Senovo was straining forward against the grip on his hair, reaching out to lap at the angry red tip. I plastered myself a bit tighter against Andoc's back, watching avidly.

"As long as you keep your teeth covered and aren't too shy about it, sucking cock is almost guaranteed to please a man," Andoc said in a rough voice. "Senovo takes a certain pride in his technique, though…"

Andoc was slowly feeding his cock to the priest, who closed his eyes with evident enjoyment. Senovo choked a bit when he was about two-thirds of the way down the shaft, and I realized with a shiver that the head of Andoc's prick must have hit the back of his throat. I watched in awe when, rather than pull back, Senovo swallowed around the intrusion a couple of times, relaxing his neck and jaw before sliding forward the last few inches until his nose was buried in Andoc's dark pubic hair.

All of the tension seemed to bleed from Senovo's muscles. Only the slight jerk of his chest as his lungs tried to drag air past the cock lodged in his throat marred his perfect stillness. By contrast, I could feel Andoc's muscles quivering under my arms as he fought to stay still. His hand held Senovo in position as the priest worked his tongue against the underside of Andoc's prick, his jaw muscles rippling.

The flesh between my legs throbbed hot and insistent at the sight. Finally, Andoc pulled Senovo back by the hair, and the priest's wet gasp was followed immediately by a muffled groan of disappointment. Senovo sucked hard on the tip of Andoc's shaft, his tongue curling around the hard flesh as he bobbed his head in shallow movements, guided by the hand controlling him.

Letting my own hands and lips wander, I ran my fingers lightly over Andoc's chest, feathering across the bruises left by Varanis' shield and skirting the edges of the shallow cut from her sword. I let my palms slide over his nipples as Senovo worshipped his cock, feeling them pebble underneath my touch. Experimentally, I scraped one lightly with a ragged fingernail. Immediately, I was rewarded with Andoc's choked curse and Senovo's pleased moan as Andoc's hips snapped forward, driving him further into Senovo's willing mouth.

"He wants you deeper," I whispered into Andoc's ear. Senovo's dark, dilated eyes met mine, giving me the courage to keep talking. "He wants you to fuck his mouth properly until he forgets everything except the smell and taste of you."

"*Carivel*. Gods above," Andoc groaned. I scratched across his other nipple, lowering my head to nip my way down the side of his neck, and was rewarded with another jerk of his hips as Andoc whispered, "*Caradi...*"

I froze; my breath caught in my lungs at the unexpected endearment.

Amadi. Worthy of love.

Caradi. Worthy of care and respect. A variant of my name… my *real* name.

I couldn't breathe for a moment. As I forced myself back under control, I was aware of Senovo looking up at me with perfect understanding.

"Say it again," I said, tightening my arms even as Senovo took advantage of Andoc's distraction to swallow him to the root once more. "Then give your *amadi* what he needs."

"*Caradi!*" Andoc gasped, and pulled Senovo back by the hair only to fuck into his throat again, and again, and again. Senovo gave himself over with utter abandon, his expression as serene as if he were gazing upon the faces of all the gods and goddesses. I clung to Andoc, lost in a heady mix of desire and burgeoning love as I kissed every bit of him that I could reach, running my hands over the tense muscles of his stomach.

Before long, his hips stuttered, losing their rhythm. With a groan, Andoc's spine arched like a bow and he came, spurting his release into Senovo's mouth until he couldn't swallow any more and it dribbled down his chin in pearly globs.

Andoc shuddered in my arms, breathing as hard as if he'd just run a footrace. He curled further forward, the hand holding Senovo in place gentling to a caress. Senovo rested his cheek on Andoc's thigh, eyes closed, suckling gently even as Andoc's flesh softened in his mouth. Eventually, he pulled off with a faint pop, drawing a final shiver from the spent man.

"Dear *gods*," Andoc said faintly, and I squeezed my arms tighter around him in response. "Sorry... *sorry*. I need to—"

He made to rise and move toward Senovo, who was sitting back on his heels looking soft and relaxed. Andoc reeled a bit when his muscles didn't cooperate as he expected.

"Sit for a minute," I told him firmly. "Just tell me what I need to do for him."

Andoc blinked, obviously struggling to drag his thoughts back into focus. "Untie his legs. Check his arms to make sure the blood is flowing all right. If it is, leave them tied and help him up onto the bed."

"Got it," I said, pressing a final kiss to his shoulder.

Senovo was a subdued, pliant figure as I knelt next to him. He leaned into me trustingly, and remembering the way Andoc had reassured him the other night after he'd stopped fighting the ropes, I took a few moments to run my hands over his soft skin with firm, even strokes. I traced the lines of his shoulders and arms, checking the color of his hands in the flickering firelight to make sure the ropes weren't too tight.

Sliding my hands down his chest and over his stomach, I traced one of the ropes binding his ankles to his upper thighs, following it inward, close to where his small prick still hung limp, despite the evident pleasure he'd experienced while sucking Andoc off.

"Don't touch his sac," Andoc said quietly from the bed. "It still pains him sometimes, and the associations aren't good, as you can imagine. The prick is all right, though."

I nodded, once again feeling a surge of deep, burning anger at the people who had done this to Senovo against his will. Pushing it down, I focused instead on the feeling of having him here, now, so relaxed and unguarded under my hands. Avoiding the flap of wrinkled skin where his stones should have hung, I traced his cock with the tip of my finger, fascinated by the way it twitched faintly under my touch. I cupped it in my palm, and Senovo sighed out in contentment. The column of flesh stiffened a bit under my tentative ministrations, only to soften again almost immediately.

Mindful of Andoc's instructions, I moved my attention back to the rope, untying the knots that held Senovo in a kneeling position. When he was free, I tossed it aside and guided him into a loose sprawl against me. Unable to resist, I lapped up the dribble of Andoc's release that trailed down Senovo's chin, rolling it around on my tongue to explore the bitter saltiness of it. Senovo nuzzled closer, seeking a kiss, and I licked into his mouth, chasing more of the salt-sea flavor.

Kissing Senovo lost none of its allure when he was in this soft, submissive place, and I had to force myself to pull away. When I did, my eyes were drawn to Andoc's love bite on his shoulder. My desire surged, and I indulged my earlier fantasy of fitting my fingers to the livid bruise and pressing down. Instead of crying out, though,

Senovo went limp against me — all except his prick, which twitched and filled slightly.

With a growl of lust, I shifted him in my arms until I could bite down on his other shoulder, sucking my own mark to the surface while I wrapped a hand around his half-hard cock. At that, Senovo did groan — his voice roughened by the throat fucking he'd received earlier.

"You two are going to kill me," Andoc said from the bed. "Get him up here now, before I'm forced to come down there and make you."

The prospect of Andoc *making me* was enough to have me breathless and — impossibly — even wetter than before. I worried at Senovo's shoulder, dragging a final shudder from him as another pulse of moisture dribbled down my thigh. Guiding him into a more upright position, I levered myself to my feet and helped him stand on unsteady legs. Fortunately, the bed was right in front of us, and it was mostly a matter of spilling him into it. Andoc had roused himself enough to drag Senovo closer to the center and position him on his side, facing me. Once Senovo was safely spooned against him, eyes closed in contentment, Andoc reached over and picked up the little jar of grease Senovo had used earlier.

"I told you earlier that I'd show you how to help me take him apart," he said. "He's ready for it now, I think. With eunuchs, it's not so much that they can't feel sexual pleasure. More that they don't miss it when they don't have it, and tend not to think about it when they aren't actually in bed with someone."

"I felt him start to get stiff in my hand just now," I said, intrigued.

Andoc nodded. "You and I can get excited just by seeing someone we'd like to fuck, or thinking about sex. He needs our hands and mouths on him before he can really get going."

"You said earlier that I could suck him?" I asked eagerly, stroking my fingers over Senovo's scalp as he lay cradled between us.

"You suck, I'll fuck," Andoc said, a smile tugging at his lips as he waggled greasy fingers at me.

Senovo groaned against my shoulder, evidently back from wherever he'd been floating earlier. "*Really*, Andoc?" he said, his voice still gravelly. "I'm going to pretend I didn't hear that."

"Hush, you," I told him, affection threatening to bubble over inside my chest once more. "This is all part of my education. And, as you reminded us earlier, you're a priest."

"But just for that, you're not to come until I give you permission," Andoc added. He pulled Senovo's head back into an uncomfortable arch. "Understood?"

As quickly as that, Senovo's eyes glazed over, and he was back in the quiet place that only Andoc seemed to be able to send him.

"I could watch that all day," I said.

"Oh, it gets better, believe me," Andoc said. He arranged himself at Senovo's hips and lifted the priest's top leg, resting the ankle on his shoulder to keep him spread open. "Here, Carivel—lie on your side facing his feet. You can use his thigh for a pillow while you suck him."

I eagerly shuffled into position, scooting Senovo's bottom leg forward until I could get a good angle at his cock while resting my head on the smooth skin of his inner thigh. At first I was unsure quite what to do with my legs, but then it occurred to me to return the favor, and I rearranged us until we were mirroring each other, Senovo resting his head on my leg and nuzzling eagerly against my damp curls.

"Very nice," Andoc approved. "Now… let me just—"

With Senovo's upper leg raised and resting on Andoc's shoulder, I had a pretty clear view of things if I craned my neck a bit. From my vantage point only a few inches away, I watched Andoc press a greased finger into Senovo's tight opening. The priest moaned against my cunt as his small cock filled, growing until the head poked out of the foreskin and nudged against my lips. I kissed the tip, darting my tongue out to taste.

"Remember," Andoc said, "no teeth, and don't try to take more than you can manage. All good?"

"Mmm… very," I replied, as Senovo nuzzled between my legs again.

Andoc twisted his wrist and Senovo grunted, his prick twitching hard. I kissed it again and slid my lips over the tip, exploring the shape with my tongue and breathing in the smell of musk. Already, I was beginning to understand what Senovo saw in this. As Andoc worked him slowly open, I concentrated on taking more, letting Senovo slide deeper and breathing through my nose. I still had a decent view of what Andoc was doing and I watched, fascinated. After a few minutes, Andoc added a second finger and scissored them back and forth, stretching Senovo's fluttering opening while I hollowed my cheeks to suck as I'd seen him do to Andoc earlier.

Senovo's breath was coming in shallow pants that huffed against my own dripping flesh, making me shiver. Every once in awhile he would lap at me or slide his nose along my inner lips, making me hum around him in pleasure.

"Here's the really good part," Andoc said, scooping up more grease and pressing a third finger alongside the other two. "Brace yourself, now —"

He changed the angle of his wrist, the muscles of his forearm working as he moved his fingers inside Senovo's body as if searching for something. The result was dramatic — the priest stiffened and *keened*, writhing around the fingers penetrating him and jerking his arms against the bonds trapping them behind his back. Andoc clamped his free arm around the thigh of Senovo's raised leg to keep him in place and I grabbed his hip, further restraining him.

Andoc set up an unforgiving rhythm, never letting up as he slid his fingers across whatever it was inside Senovo that made him jerk his hips against our hold, trying to drive himself alternately back onto the invading fingers and forward into my mouth. I worked at letting him in deeper until I was taking all but the final inch or so, keeping my lips carefully over my teeth. My jaw and neck were starting to ache, but it was worth that and more to watch Senovo mindlessly chase after the pleasure we were bringing him.

"Do you need to come, *amadi*?" Andoc asked solicitously, when Senovo's gasps started sounding suspiciously like sobs.

The priest nodded urgently, apparently beyond words—I could feel the motion where his head was still pillowed on my thigh.

"Hmm. Such a pity you don't have permission yet," said Andoc, and added a fourth finger.

Senovo jerked in my mouth and cried out, but miraculously did not come. I gave him an extra-hard suck just to see what would happen, and, yes, that time the noise was *definitely* a sob.

"Tell you what," Andoc said. "You make Carivel come with your hard prick stuffed in her mouth, and maybe we'll let you have your release after she's done."

Senovo's lips were clamped around my aching nub before I could even think about bracing for it. All of his earlier methodical technique was completely gone—he sucked and laved at the tender flesh desperately, nipping and licking for all he was worth. I cried out around the cock in my mouth, completely unprepared for the landslide of pleasure crashing over me. In retaliation, I sucked Senovo down to the root, trying to drag him with me as I plummeted headfirst over the edge.

I was vaguely aware of Andoc twisting his fingers and saying, "That's it, *amadi*. Come for us now."

Senovo shouted something wordless against my oversensitive flesh, drawing a final shudder from me as he swelled and pulsed against my tongue. A tiny spurt of fluid squirted onto the back of my tongue and I swallowed it—nothing compared to the load that Andoc had choked him with earlier. I continued to suck Senovo's softening cock lazily as Andoc's fingers milked a few more tremors of pleasure from his body. His breath was hot against me as he gradually subsided into a limp, shivering mess between us. Though, to be fair to him, I wasn't doing much better.

I gave him a last, lingering lick and let his soft flesh slide out of my mouth, the thought of moving any further completely laughable at the moment. Andoc carefully pulled his fingers out and wiped his greasy hand on the rag—somewhat awkwardly since he was still holding Senovo's top leg up to keep it from crushing my head.

"Roll over," he said, giving my shoulder a nudge until I rolled onto my back with a heartfelt groan. He lowered Senovo's leg and reached up to untie his arms; the priest remained completely oblivious, still lost in the afterglow. Apparently unconcerned, Andoc rose to set the rope aside and retrieve the blanket from the floor. He urged me to scoot around until I was facing the right direction on the bed. Senovo immediately burrowed into my arms, and Andoc looked down at us both with an expression of proprietary pleasure.

"Gorgeous, the pair of you," he said, stroking my hair.

"I want to suck you off next," I murmured, already half-asleep.

"Soon, but not tonight," he said with a hint of amusement. "Even if I weren't too sore to go again, I think both of you are pretty much done at the moment. Here—budge over."

Crowding me even closer to Senovo, Andoc crawled in behind me and curled his body around mine, pulling a blanket over all three of us. He threw an arm over me to rest his hand on Senovo's shoulder protectively, and let out a deep sigh of contentment.

Tomorrow, Andoc would ride home to Draebard. His meeting with Chief Volya would determine our future—and possibly the future of Eburos, as the Alyrion Empire stood poised at our borders. Now, though, I was safe in the arms of the two men who had become more important to me than anything else. With Andoc guarding my back, and Senovo curled trustingly in my arms, I slid down into a deep, untroubled sleep.

finis

Carivel's adventures continue in *The Horse Mistress: Book 2.*

Curious about Andoc and Senovo's history? Sign up at http://www.rasteffan.com/tec/ and get the free e-book prequel to *The Horse Mistress* series delivered to your email inbox.

www.ingramcontent.com/pod-product-compliance
Lightning Source LLC
Chambersburg PA
CBHW031013190726

48286CB00003BA/818